"I t...

Rache... ....., ... but powerless to do anything about it. Time seemed to stand still. She looked at Daniel as through a haze, saw his face alight with expectancy, and knew she ought to make some sort of response. "You—what?" she croaked.

"I know it's a bit sudden," Daniel began, "but when you think about it, it makes perfect sense."

Rachel stood motionless, waiting for him to explain how it could possibly make any sense at all.

"You've been knocking yourself out to keep things going and get the money you need to pay off the bank," he said. "You're working hard. Too hard. I have an idea that can help both of us. If you marry me, I can make the payment for you, and you can keep the farm."

Rachel's eyes narrowed. "You said it would help us both. What do you get out of it?"

Daniel stuck his hands in his pants pockets and swallowed. "Plenty. A home and a family and—"

"And my father's farm!" she shouted, hot tears spilling over to course down her cheeks. Decent and sincere she'd thought him. Had there never been an honorable man in the world save her father?

Daniel spread his hands, a look of bewilderment crossing his face. "Well, sure, I'd work the farm—"

"Leave me alone!" She bolted into the house.

CAROL COX is a native of Arizona whose time is devoted to being a pastor's wife, homeschool mom to her teenage son and young daughter, church pianist, youth worker, and 4-H leader. She loves activities she can share with her family in addition to her own pursuits in reading, gardening, crafts, and local history. Carol and her family make their home in northern Arizona.

HEARTSONG PRESENTS

Books by Carol Cox
HP264—Journey Toward Home
HP344—The Measure of a Man

Season
of Hope

Carol Cox

Heartsong Presents

Rejoicing in hope; patient in tribulation;
continuing instant in prayer.
ROMANS 12:12

A note from the author:
*I love to hear from my readers! You may correspond with me
by writing:*

**Carol Cox
Author Relations
PO Box 719
Uhrichsville, OH 44683**

ISBN 1-58660-383-3

SEASON OF HOPE

All Scripture quotations, unless noted, are taken from the King
James Version of the Bible.

All of the characters and events in this book are fictitious. Any
resemblance to actual persons, living or dead, or to actual events
is purely coincidental.

Cover design by Joyclyne Bouchard

PRINTED IN THE U.S.A.

one

"Come in, Rachel. Have a seat."

Rachel Canfield slid into the dark leather chair facing Ben Murphy's massive oak desk, her back straight, chin up, trying to exude an air of confidence she didn't feel. The bank manager's office was a familiar setting. Goodness knew, she'd been in there often enough with her father, but having to conduct business on her own gave the room an odd sense of unfamiliarity today.

"I want to tell you again how sorry I am about your father's accident."

Rachel nodded briefly, appreciating the sentiment, but not wanting to deal with the fresh wound of her loss right then. She cleared her throat, then hesitated, lacing her fingers into a white-knuckled knot. What was wrong with her? Ben Murphy had been her father's friend for all the time they'd lived in Arizona Territory. In her present hardship, she knew she could count on him to be an ally. She had absolutely no need to be nervous.

Ben leaned forward, giving her an encouraging smile. Rachel breathed a quick prayer for courage, squared her shoulders, and got right to the point. "The farm is doing well. *Very* well," she added for emphasis. "I fully expect to make a better profit than ever this year." Ben nodded, obviously pleased, and Rachel drew in a long, shaky breath. She had

5

just given him the good news. Now for the hard part.

"Unfortunately, we've had a good many extra expenses, what with the doctor and the. . .the funeral and all." Rachel's voice shook, and she pressed her lips together for a moment, trying to regain her composure. "I'd like an extension on our loan payment—just for a few months," she added hastily as Ben's smile faded and his eyebrows drew together. "Just until we catch up a little bit." Her voice trailed off, and she sat speechless, hating the way her lower lip quivered, but powerless to stop it.

Ben looked at his hands, at his inkwell, at the Seth Thomas clock on the wall—anywhere but at Rachel.

What was going on? The Canfields had always paid their debts and always would. Ben knew that. Why did he suddenly look so unfriendly? Why did he refuse to look Rachel in the eye?

"I'm afraid I can't do that." His eyes focused on a Currier and Ives print across the room.

Rachel's breath came in short, jerky gasps. "But–but why?" she faltered. "You know you'll get the money."

Ben ran a finger back and forth inside his collar. "If it were up to me, Rachel, you'd get the extension. Your father was a man of honor, and you've always followed him that way. But the board of directors has already met to discuss your loan. They don't believe two young women can keep the place up by themselves, so if you and your sister have any problem making this year's payment—any at all—I'm supposed to hold you strictly to the terms of the agreement."

"I don't believe it!" Rachel slammed her palms down on the polished desk top, relishing the way the blow made her hands sting. The pain shocked her out of her confusion and helped her marshal her thoughts. "Do you mean to tell me that after all the years I've worked with my father, Doc Howell and Ed Silverton don't think I'm capable of making a go of the place now that he's gone?"

"It's—it's not Doc and Ed exactly," Ben mumbled.

"Then who?" Rachel demanded. "Who's left? Everyone around here knows I'm a hard worker and that I know what I'm doing. That makes me a good investment, Ben. Who would want to see me fail?"

Ben stared miserably at the rug as if fascinated by the floral pattern. "I don't know that Hiram *wants* to see you fail, exactly. . . ."

"Hiram? Hiram Bradshaw?" Rachel's voice rose to a screech. "What does he have to do with this?"

"He just invested in the bank, Rachel. He's on the board of directors now." Ben's gaze met hers at last. "In fact, he's the biggest investor in the bank, so he has the biggest say in what we do. And what he said about you was that I was to give you no leeway on this. None whatsoever."

"What about all the time you and Pa spent together?" Rachel hurled the question at him. "Didn't his friendship mean anything to you?"

Ben squirmed, looking more like an errant schoolboy caught in a misdeed than the manager of a financial institution. "I wish it were up to me," he said, shaking his head. "I really do."

Rachel rose from her chair and leaned as far over the desk as her five feet five inches would allow. "All right, Ben Murphy." She ground out the words. "We worked hard to build that farm up out of nothing but a hole in the forest—too hard to let it slip away to a scoundrel like Hiram Bradshaw. I don't know just how we'll manage it, but you can expect to have the full two hundred dollars right here on your desk December 15, and not a day later." She stood up and smoothed her skirt with trembling hands, preparing to make a sweeping exit. Ben's quiet voice stopped her.

"It's not two hundred, Rachel." At her sharp glance, he squirmed again. "Your father borrowed more money for mining equipment last spring. He signed a paper, promising to pay that in full, along with the loan amount. You'll need to come up with three hundred dollars."

Rachel's knees gave way, and she sagged back into the chair.

"Your father anticipated getting enough from this year's crop and his mine to pay it all off with no problem," Ben explained with a sympathetic look. "I know he never dreamed he'd leave you girls in the lurch like this."

Three hundred dollars! Rachel's mind whirled crazily, trying to calculate ways and means of coming up with that amount. Stiffly, she rose to her feet once more. "Then that's what you'll have," she said through taut lips. "I don't know how, but you'll get your money, Ben. Every penny of it."

Ignoring the pitying disbelief in the banker's eyes, Rachel pivoted and stalked out the door, her back ramrod straight and her head held high. No one, least of all Hiram Bradshaw, would take their land from them. And no one was going to see her look the least bit concerned about it! She climbed into the wagon seat and gathered the reins in one fluid motion.

≥•

Thumb Butte. Granite Mountain. Williams Peak. The familiar landmarks stood in the same places they had occupied for thousands of years. Rachel could gauge her location within a hundred yards just by a quick glance at her surroundings. Nothing had changed outwardly, yet everything was different, just because of Pa's passing.

Rachel viewed the passing landscape with shock-dimmed eyes, barely noticing the wagon turn when the road curved in the direction of Iron Springs and home.

How much longer would she and Violet be able to call it home? Her brave declaration to Ben Murphy had sounded fine inside the bank, but how on earth could she possibly come up with three hundred dollars in the space of three months?

"That prideful streak of yours is going to land you in trouble some day, Rachel." She could hear Pa's voice as clearly as if he'd been riding in the wagon seat next to her. How she wished she could turn and see him sitting there! She needed his calm guidance now, more than ever.

Rachel groaned aloud, and the wheel horse flicked one ear back, checking out the unexpected sound. With their lives suddenly turned upside down, raising two hundred dollars would have been challenge enough, but *three* hundred? "It's impossible," she informed the horses. "Utterly impossible."

With God all things are possible. Rachel gasped and spun about on the wagon seat, her heart pounding wildly. No one but she and the plodding horses were in sight. " 'With God all things are possible,' " she whispered, the verse from the Gospels sounding clear and fresh. "All things. Not everything but getting enough money to keep Hiram Bradshaw's greedy fingers off our land. *All* things." A way existed, and God would provide it. All she had to do was find out what that way might be.

The vague outline of a plan had begun to form in her mind by the time she turned off the road and into the farmyard. Wanting to share the idea with her sister before she lost her train of thought, she pulled the horses to a stop in front of the house and hurriedly dismounted from the wagon. "Violet!"

she called. There was no answer. "Violet?" she tried again, louder this time.

A quick glance from the front door showed no sign of her sister. Rachel stood on the porch, hands on her hips, and tapped her foot impatiently. Wasn't that always the way? Here she had a perfectly wonderful notion just waiting to be shared, and Violet was nowhere to be found.

Rachel took a deep breath, ready to call out again, when a wail burst forth from the barn. "Violet!" she shrieked and raced across the hard-packed dirt, skirts held high, visions of mayhem flashing through her mind.

"Where are you?" she hollered when she arrived, panting, at the wide-open double door.

The dreadful yowling erupted again, just overhead. Rachel's head snapped back to scan the hayloft. What could her sister be doing up there? And what was happening to her to cause her to produce that inhuman sound? Rachel mounted the ladder leading to the loft. "I'm coming, Violet," she called breathlessly. "Just hang on."

"Thank goodness you're here." Violet's legs swung precariously near Rachel's nose to dangle over the edge of the loft. Bits of hay adorned her glossy dark hair and her skirt was rumpled, but otherwise she seemed in good condition—and remarkably unruffled for someone making such an unearthly noise.

Rachel stared openmouthed at her younger sister. "What on earth is going on?" she demanded, panic making her voice harsh. "You sounded like you were being murdered."

Violet blinked in surprise at her sister's accusing tone, then grinned. "Not me," she said, laughter gurgling in her throat. "Come on up." She scooted to one side and helped Rachel scramble from the top of the ladder to the loft.

Rachel wrinkled her nose at the hay dust she stirred up. She slapped at her skirt and sneezed violently when a cloud of the fine dust assailed her nostrils. "All right. What—*choo!*—is making that horrible noise?" Violet pointed to one corner. "I don't see any—any—ah–ahh—" The discordant wail sounded again, cutting her off in mid sneeze.

"It's Molly," Violet explained, indicating the gray tabby cat that crouched against the wall, swiping her paw at a large orange-and-white tom. "Well, not Molly exactly," she said, watching the male visitor tilt his head back for another round of impassioned caterwauling.

"It's that tomcat of Jeb McCurdy's again!" Rachel fumed. "And after I've told him a dozen times to keep the mangy thing at home." Snatching the amorous cat by the scruff of the neck, she carried him down the ladder, ignoring his loud objections. "Where's that old sewing basket?" she asked Violet, who had followed her down, carrying Molly in one arm.

Violet reached behind a pile of grain sacks and pulled out the covered basket, which Rachel snatched gladly, depositing the lovesick tom inside and fastening the lid securely before he had a chance to escape. "There," she announced triumphantly. "That ought to hold him until I get him to McCurdy's place." She stalked off to the wagon, where the horses still stood in their harness.

Preparing to swing the basket onto the seat, Rachel paused to shade her eyes and peered at a distant figure coming toward them on the road. "Talk about timing!" she crowed. "There's Jeb McCurdy in his buggy now." With a grim smile, she grabbed the basket and strode off to intercept their neighbor.

Shielding her eyes with one hand, she waved her other arm in a wide arc. McCurdy slowed his horse to a walk, staring curiously. "Need some help, Miss Rachel?" he asked congenially, shooting a stream of tobacco juice neatly to one side of the buggy.

"What I need, Mr. McCurdy, is for you to keep your wayward animal at home."

"My what?" McCurdy rubbed his grizzled chin with a work-worn hand, a puzzled frown creasing his forehead.

"This wanton feline of yours." Rachel raised the basket and shook it menacingly in the surprised farmer's face, bringing indignant yowls of protest from the prisoner within. "I have asked you repeatedly to keep him from wandering onto our property, but he was back again today, tormenting our poor Molly."

The owner of the treacherous tom cast a bewildered look at Violet, who stood nearby holding Molly, then back at the avenging fury before him. "But I thought your sister's name was—" A second glance at the cat nestling comfortably in Violet's arms brought illumination to his weather-beaten face, and a muffled chuckle escaped his lips. "Molly—she'd be your cat, would she?"

"Of course she is," Rachel snapped. Her feelings raw after learning of the possible loss of the farm, she found a certain satisfaction in venting her pent-up anger. "The poor thing was cowering in a corner, trying to fend him off. Who knows what might have happened if we hadn't intervened?"

"Who knows, indeed?" McCurdy mumbled, rubbing a hand across his mouth.

Rachel pressed on, heedless of the interruption. "I want your word—your solemn word, Mr. McCurdy—that you will keep that beast on your own property from now on. We have enough to do to keep the place running without having to deal with the attention of unwanted intruders." She folded her arms and fixed McCurdy with a severe look, daring him to argue.

The faintest curve tilted one corner of McCurdy's mouth. "Has it occurred to you, Miss Rachel, that his attentions might not be totally unwanted? By Molly, that is," he hastened to add.

Rachel's fist tightened on the basket handle, fighting the urge to fling it, cat and all, straight at her neighbor and knock that infuriating smirk right off his face. "Mr. McCurdy," she said in icy tones, "I assure you that none of us, Molly included, have the slightest desire to entertain that creature. Please take your appalling animal and keep him at home. Or at least away from here!"

McCurdy caught the basket Rachel thrust at him and fumbled with the lid. "Oh, no," she told him, replacing the latch firmly. "Keep him in there until you get him home. You can return the basket later."

Nodding agreement, McCurdy snapped the reins and started his horse down the road. A rasping laugh floated back over his shaking shoulders to where Rachel stood glaring after him.

Hot tears stung her eyes, and she balled her hands into fists. How dare that old reprobate make fun of a serious situation! No wonder his cat behaved the way he did, she told herself; he was a reflection of his owner. Sniffling, she whirled purposefully toward the house and walked headlong into a tree that hadn't been there earlier.

two

"Ow!" Blinded by tears of pain, Rachel doubled over, with both hands clamped to her nose. Voices, one Violet's, one she had never heard before, floated above her.

"Rachel, are you all right? What happened?"

"I'm not sure." This from the strange voice, a mellow baritone. "She just ran smack into me." Strong hands took hold of Rachel's shoulders with a firm yet gentle grasp. "Are you hurt? Let's see."

Rachel raised her head slowly, still pressing her throbbing nose, to see two blurry figures before her. Blinking rapidly to clear her vision, she focused on the tall, sandy-haired man standing next to Violet. "Who are you?" she asked, her voice muffled by her hands. She threw a look at her sister, silently demanding an explanation.

Violet gave a nervous laugh. "We have company," she said helpfully. "You didn't hear us talking, because you were, ah, busy with Mr. McCurdy."

Jeb McCurdy! Rachel felt her cheeks flame, remembering the dressing-down she had given the grizzled miner. She must have sounded like a fishwife! What must this man, whoever he was, think of her? She turned back to him, pulling her hands from her face, and heard Violet gasp. Looking down, Rachel saw the bright red blood staining her fingers and a blotch of the same color on the front of the stranger's white shirt.

Mortified, she clapped her hands to her cheeks, regretting

14

the action the instant she felt the sticky warmth from her fingers. She squeezed her eyes shut, wishing with all her might the man would be gone when she opened them again. Instead, he still stood before her, holding out a snowy handkerchief. Rachel took it without a word and held it to her nose, gratified that the bleeding seemed to have slowed.

"I'm Rachel Canfield," she said through the folds of fabric. "I take it you've already met my sister, Violet."

"Daniel Moore," replied the stranger. He held out his right hand, then appeared to reconsider and tucked it into his pocket. His gaze swept over Rachel from head to toe, and she felt as though she'd been appraised by his deep green eyes and found wanting. "I apologize for coming up on you like that. I thought you had finished your conversation, and I was coming to introduce myself. I didn't realize you were. . . preoccupied."

Rachel flinched at the reminder of her outburst. "I'm the one who should apologize, running into you like that. Look what I've done to your shirt! And your handkerchief," she added lamely, staring at the crimson-spotted square of fabric in her hand.

"Mr. Moore was a friend of Pa's," Violet said happily.

Then why haven't I seen him before? The day's upheaval made Rachel leery of putting her confidence in a total stranger.

"I thought maybe we could ask him to supper," Violet went on. Rachel opened her mouth to refuse but stopped when she saw the pleading look on her sister's face. What could it hurt? She didn't trust Daniel Moore—she didn't trust much of anyone at the moment—but she did owe him something after ruining his shirt. Besides, she could tell that entertaining a friend of their father's meant a lot to Violet.

"Will you join us, Mr. Moore?" she asked, attempting a gracious smile, but the taut feeling of dried blood on her cheeks reminded her of how she must look, and the smile faded. When he hesitated, she hastened to add, "If we get your shirt in some cold water right away, we might be able to get the blood stain out before it has time to set."

Daniel looked ruefully at his shirt front and gave Rachel a crooked smile. "I don't want to be a bother, but I did have something to discuss with you. That might be the best way to do it, if it's all right with you."

ॐ

Daniel sat at the dining table, wearing one of Ike Canfield's shirts. His own sat soaking in a bowl of cold water Rachel had drawn. He wriggled his shoulders, trying to stretch the fabric a bit. Ike had been as tall as Daniel, but lean as a whipcord. Ike's arms had been shorter too Daniel thought with amusement, looking down at his own tanned wrists extending well past the ends of the sleeves.

He scooted the chair sideways and stretched his long legs out before him, wondering how much longer Rachel would be. She had caught sight of her reflection in the front window when they entered the house, and Daniel had been hard-pressed not to laugh out loud at her strangled cry of dismay. After putting his shirt in to soak and loaning him one of Ike's, she had immediately dashed off to repair the damage, Daniel supposed. Violet had gone out to feed the chickens right after that, leaving Daniel very much alone. He fidgeted again, wanting to get the upcoming interview over with.

Smoothing her light brown hair back from her face, Rachel walked into the kitchen, her expression contrite. She pulled out two loaves of bread and a sharp knife and began cutting the bread into even slices.

"Exactly how did you know my father?" The words tumbled out abruptly. "I mean, I never heard him speak of you. . . ." She pressed her lips together and eyed Daniel expectantly.

"My mining claim was next to his," he answered.

Rachel's hands froze in midslice. "Then you were there when the beam fell on him?" Her eyes widened, and the knife wavered in her hand.

Daniel shook his head miserably. "I was gone that day, that whole week, in fact. I had to go over to Camp Verde on business, and I didn't get back until it was all over. I didn't even make it to the funeral," he said in a dull voice. "If I'd been around, I might have heard the commotion and gotten to him in time."

And if you had, he told himself, *you might be sitting here now having supper with the whole family, instead of with two girls who have been left alone in the world.* It was possible, he reasoned. Old Ike had extended an invitation often enough. But for someone as skittish around women as Daniel, the mere mention of two unmarried daughters in the household had been enough to make him keep his distance.

He watched Rachel's mobile face as she digested the news that her father might not have died if only he, Daniel Webster Moore, had been close by. If he hadn't made the spontaneous trip to Camp Verde. If he'd been around to hear and lend a helping hand, they might never have suffered this loss. And he would not now be in this unpleasant position.

This wouldn't be easy; he could see that already. Ike's description of his daughters had been remarkably accurate. "Violet's a frail little thing," he had told Daniel more than once. "Not sickly, mind you, just not sturdy like her sister. She takes after her mother, God rest her soul—dreamy and gentle, always concerned about the other person's feelings.

"Rachel, on the other hand," he would continue, "has an independent streak a mile wide. Nothing wrong with that in itself, but once she sets out to do something, that stubborn pride of hers won't let her change direction. And feisty? My land, that girl has a temper! Rachel isn't one you want to cross without a rock-solid reason."

Ike had been right on target. Daniel could see that, even after his brief acquaintance with the sisters, and it wouldn't make his self-appointed task one bit simpler. Violet would probably accept his offer as the sensible solution it was. It was Rachel who worried him.

Taking a deep breath, he decided to plunge right in. No use beating around the bush with this one. "You're going to need some help on this farm," he began. "You still have the corn and beans to get in and the late vegetables to harvest, not to mention needing to cut firewood and plow the fields before winter. Your father was a good man, one of the best. He helped me out more than once, and I'd like to do something to repay the favor." He glanced at Rachel, who eyed him narrowly.

"Just exactly what did you have in mind?" she asked in a tight voice.

"I can give you a hand with all of that. I'm a hard worker, and I'd like to do it in memory of your pa."

Rachel seemed to turn the proposition over in her mind while she melted lard in the skillet. To most, Daniel knew, it would seem a generous offer from a friend. But this stubborn, proud woman would likely be rankled if she felt beholden to a stranger.

The door swung open to admit Violet, cheeks tinged a rosy pink from the nip in the air, the hem of her apron gathered in her hands. "Can you believe it? I found six more eggs when I fed the hens." She removed the eggs from her apron and set them gently on the counter, blithely unaware of the undercurrents in the room.

Rachel didn't answer her sister but swung around to face Daniel. "I appreciate your offer, Mr. Moore, but I believe God has already shown me a plan to keep things going here. We're going to be strapped for cash until our bank loan is paid off, so I couldn't pay you, and I certainly couldn't allow you to work for us for nothing. Thank you for your generosity, but the answer is no."

A knot formed in Daniel's stomach. It hadn't been easy for him to convince himself to approach Ike's daughters. Women, in Daniel's experience, were better left alone. But Ike had been a good neighbor—more than that, he had saved his bacon the time he'd run off those Yavapai Apaches that had Daniel pinned down. In Daniel's book, a debt like that couldn't go unpaid. He hadn't been there to help Ike, but he could step in now to do what he could for Ike's family. And Rachel seemed ready to throw his offer away without even discussing it.

In the six weeks since Ike's death, the girls had done a remarkable job of keeping the place going. The fields were well tended, and the livestock were in obviously good shape. It had probably been good for them to keep busy with a regular routine. But now they faced the prospect of bringing in the harvest, where they would make the bulk of their income. If that wasn't done right and on time, all the other hard work would have been for nothing.

Daniel noted the determined set of Rachel's chin, and the knot in his stomach tightened. Did she really believe she and her sister could do it on their own? He shook his head in reluctant admiration. Her father had her figured, all right—independence and stubborn pride enough for three people.

He nodded, outwardly accepting her decision. "It's your

choice," he said. "Have it your way." Under his breath he added, "For now." He had a debt to pay, and a stubborn streak of his own.

Visibly relieved at his acquiescence, Rachel turned her attention to Violet. "Go ahead and add those eggs to the ones you brought in this morning and cook them up, will you?"

Violet rolled her eyes. "Eggs again?"

"We have to do something with them. Those hens are laying faster than we can use them up. Even with the ones you keep sneaking to Molly," Rachel added, clearly suppressing a chuckle when an embarrassed flush stained her sister's cheeks. "I hope you like eggs, Mr. Moore," she called over her shoulder, then frowned. "What's the matter?"

Daniel's mouth hung open in utter astonishment. "You're trying to get *rid* of your eggs?" he asked, stunned.

A crease appeared between Rachel's eyebrows. "It's not that we're ungrateful; we just have more than we can possibly use. What's wrong?"

Daniel shook his head in disbelief. "Just that most folks around here would give their eye teeth for an occasional egg, and here you are, throwing them away."

"Giving the extras to Molly isn't throwing them away," Violet retorted with a sniff.

"Wait a minute." Rachel stared at Daniel. "Do you mean you think we could sell some of these eggs?"

"Not some," Daniel corrected. "All. Why don't you take a basketful with you the next time you go into town and see what happens?"

"Maybe I will," Rachel said.

&

Rachel wrapped a length of binder twine around yet another armload of cornstalks and set the shock upright. She wiped the dampness from her brow with the back of her hand and shook her head. Even with the feel of autumn in the air, she was sweating. Harvesting the corn single-handedly made for slow going. Too slow. At this rate she wouldn't be done for weeks. And that would be much too late.

Her plan for saving the farm had seemed so simple. She and Violet would get the harvest in by themselves. Without hiring outside help, she reasoned, they'd save a lot, maybe enough to put a goodly bit toward the hundred-dollar difference in the loan amounts. They would do such a wonderful job that even the worst naysayers in town would have to admit being a woman wasn't the drawback some of them would like to believe.

Rachel knew what needed to be done and how to do it. After all, hadn't she worked with Pa on every job on the place? She still would be too if it hadn't been for the accident. If only that beam hadn't fallen just when Pa was underneath! But she was learning there was a vast difference between working alongside her father and being responsible for everything, the housework and fieldwork both.

She rolled her neck, trying to work out the kinks, and surveyed the waving corn about her. Nearly half of it had been put up. Over in the bean field, Violet moved methodically down a row, stripping the dried pods from the plants and placing them in the gunnysack she dragged along behind her. The vegetable patch, neat and weed free, was ready to yield the last crops of the season. Yes, she could be proud of all they had accomplished so far. But looking beyond that, she could also see what still needed to be done.

"I'm trying, Pa. Really, I am," she whispered, her voice catching in her throat. Tears pricked her eyes as the fresh pain of her loss tore at her once more, and she looked across the fields, aching to see her father's familiar figure striding along, a corn knife in his hand.

But Pa was gone, and no amount of longing would bring him back. An indescribable heaviness swept over her, and she felt far older than her twenty-one years. How could she possibly expect to make enough to keep her and Violet eating, much less earn enough extra to pay off the loan?

"What do I do, God?" The cry burst forth from her weary spirit. She no longer had her earthly father with her, but her heavenly Father was always near. "Even Pa had to hire workers at harvest time. And he had me to keep the house and cook for him and the crew. I've got no one except Violet. . .and You.

"If we hire men, we won't have enough money left to pay off the loan, and that miserable Hiram Bradshaw will waltz in and take the place. But if we don't get help, we'll never get it all done, and there won't be any money then, either.

"I thought I was hearing from You when I decided Violet and I would do this on our own. . .but it isn't working. We'll never get it done at this rate, and we're both so tired we're ready to drop in our tracks." She flung up her hands in despair. "All things are possible with You, but You've got to help me see the way clearly."

ટ

"If I have to eat another egg, I'll scream!" Violet's heartfelt protest rang across the kitchen.

"You'll eat them and like them, Violet Canfield. The less money we spend on food in town, the more we can set aside for the loan payment. Didn't you hear Mr. Moore the other night? Lots of people would appreciate those eggs. Be grateful."

"And I'm sick of hearing about the loan payment! That's all you seem to care about anymore." Violet's blue eyes were stormy.

"It's you I care about," Rachel retorted. "You and this farm. Pa worked hard to build it up for us, and I don't intend to lose it."

Violet crossed her arms mutinously. "At least while Pa was alive, we had decent food to eat."

Stung by the justice of Violet's remark, Rachel studied her sister's slight form with a critical eye. Violet had always been slender like their mother, but now her dress hung loosely on her slim frame—a frame that was far too thin, Rachel realized with a tinge of panic. Bread and eggs didn't make a hearty supper by any means, but they didn't have the energy to fix anything more ambitious after a day of working outdoors.

"Go on out and feed the chickens while I fix the eggs," she told Violet, trying to keep her voice level. "At least that way you won't have to watch them cooking."

Violet exited gratefully, looking contrite. Rachel cracked the eggs into a bowl, then squeezed her eyes shut and leaned her forehead against the cupboard door. "Lord, it's me again, and I need a word from You real soon. I've got to figure out a way to get the fieldwork done, and feed us decently, and tend the kitchen garden, and keep house, and. . ."

Overwhelmed, Rachel felt the hot sting of tears on her eye-lids. She bit her lower lip and shook her head, angrily dashing the tears away with the back of her hand. She couldn't afford to break down now. Maybe when all of this was over. *If it's ever over,* she thought bleakly.

Immediately, she felt a sense of shame. Five years Violet's senior, she had been responsible for her younger sister ever since their mother's death back in Missouri. With Pa gone too, who could Violet depend on if she, Rachel, gave in to despair?

With a determined tilt of her chin, she squared her shoulders and proceeded to whip the eggs into a froth, then poured them into the waiting frying pan. "Lord, I'll just keep going one step at a time. But You're going to have to show me the way."

The shuffle of footsteps and the rattle of the door latch heralded Violet's return. Rachel gave her cheeks a quick swipe with the tail of her apron to make sure no traces of dampness remained. Hearing the door open, she cleared her throat and asked brightly, "How many more of those horrible eggs did you find this time?"

"Just two." Violet slipped them onto the counter and backed away quickly. Puzzled, Rachel turned to find her sister with the egg basket on her arm and a guilty look on her face.

"And what else do you have in that basket?" she demanded.

"Oh, Rachel, he looked so pitiful, I couldn't bear to leave him outside." Holding the basket protectively, Violet scooped up a small gray object and held it out for Rachel's inspection. The little squirrel in her hand took in its new surroundings with bright eyes. Even from across the kitchen, Rachel could see that one of its back legs bent at an unnatural angle.

Rachel moved the eggs off the stove and sighed in exasperation. The last thing she needed right now was another responsibility, no matter how minor.

The squirrel chittered nervously, and Violet cuddled it close, murmuring soothing words. Memories flashed through Rachel's mind—Violet bringing home baby birds fallen from their nest. . .tending a little cottontail with a broken leg. . . She shook her head with a wry grin. This nurturing instinct was an inherent part of Violet. Just as well try to change the weather. And if it helped her get her mind off their present difficulties, why fight it?

"Make him a bed in front of the fire while I dish up supper."

three

Violet sat near the dancing flames, her fingers methodically splitting open the pods she had gathered earlier, her thumbs popping out the beans. With the squirrel curled on a bed of rags at her feet, she looked the picture of contentment.

Sitting opposite her, Rachel's hands worked just as efficiently, but inside her feelings churned. So much to do, and so little time! When Pa was alive, he and she had worked out an equitable system of sharing the responsibility for the farm. Now he was gone, and the burden was placed squarely on Rachel's shoulders. Gentle, fragile Violet couldn't be expected to carry out all Rachel's former duties. Just having her gather the bean pods had taxed her strength to the limit.

Eyeing her sister's delicate form, Rachel knew she had to do something to feed them better. But what? They couldn't spend time tending the stove when they had to be in the field harvesting. When they came in for the evening, they were far too tired to fix anything more substantial than bread and eggs. Eggs for breakfast, eggs for supper.

Rachel groaned. Violet was right—something had to change, but how? Even during the hardest parts of Rachel's life, she had never questioned God's loving care. Now, though, it was getting hard to see His hand in things.

Father, I don't mean to doubt You, but I do need an answer in a hurry. If we don't eat right, we won't be able to do all the other things we need to, so please help me figure that out right away.

One step at a time, remember? Rachel winced. She had never before addressed the Almighty so boldly, but these were desperate times. She hoped He wouldn't be offended.

Violet's voice broke into her thoughts. "Do you know where that old dynamite box of Pa's is? It would make a good home for this little fellow, but I can't remember where I saw it last."

"I think it's up in the loft." Rachel tossed her last handful of beans in the bowl between them. "I'll go look for it while you finish up." She made her way to the loft over the bedrooms, frowning as she pushed her way between cast-off boxes and keepsakes. Pa hadn't been much better than Violet about putting things away neatly, and the resulting hodgepodge had gotten out of hand. It needed a good going-over, but she wasn't likely to have time for that for quite awhile.

Rachel tried to maneuver past an old packing crate, caught her foot on something, and fell sprawling to the floor. She swiveled her head to see what had tripped her and saw the corner of a trunk protruding into the walkway. Muttering, she got to her feet and braced herself to shove the offending trunk back where it belonged, then paused and looked at it appraisingly, scattered recollections from the past appearing before her eyes like images in a scrapbook. With a grin, Rachel flung open the lid and started piling the clothing inside onto a shelf.

"Good, you're finished," she told Violet as she backed into the room, dragging the heavy chest. She tossed a stack of papers on Violet's lap. "Take these and line the trunk while I go get some hay."

"Do what?" Violet's hand paused in the act of stroking the little squirrel on her lap, and she gazed at Rachel in astonishment.

"Make it several layers thick, and don't leave any spaces."

"Rachel, are you all right?"

"Just do it. I'll be right back." Ignoring Violet's look of concern, she hustled outside.

In the barn, she stuffed armloads of grass hay into a gunnysack and returned to the house, humming merrily. "Are you finished?"

Violet, on her knees beside the trunk, looked up warily. "Will that do?" she asked, smoothing a sheet of paper into place.

Rachel looked at it judiciously. "Put one more piece in the corner. We want it to be completely sealed." Violet obeyed, keeping a cautious eye on her sister. Rachel, still humming, rummaged through the linen cupboard and pulled out an old pillowcase with a jubilant cry.

"Good job!" she told Violet. "Now stuff that with hay," she ordered, flinging the case her way.

Rachel dropped to her knees and began packing hay into the trunk. Violet watched her nervously, then grabbed fistfuls of hay and rammed them into the pillowcase with trembling hands. "Are you sure you're all right?" she asked in a shaky voice.

Rachel didn't respond but danced across the floor to the kitchen, where she lifted the large stew pot from its hook and waltzed back to the trunk with it. Nestling the pot on the bottom layer of hay, she continued to pack hay around it.

"Rachel?" Violet said in a tiny voice.

"Oh, you're done." Rachel squeezed the pillow. "Yes, that feels fine. Now stitch it closed while I finish up here."

Violet reached for the mending basket and did as she was told.

Rachel continued stuffing hay around the pot, pressing it down firmly. Taking the pillow from a bewildered Violet, she placed it on top of the pot, then closed the lid with a flourish. "And there we have it!" she cried triumphantly. When Violet didn't reply, Rachel turned to see her sister watching her with worried eyes.

"You've been working awfully hard," Violet began, putting a comforting arm around Rachel's shoulders. "Why don't you climb into bed? I'll bring you a nice, hot cup of tea."

Rachel sputtered with laughter. "Violet, you ninny! Don't you remember the hay box we used back in Missouri?" Violet shook her head slowly. "Ma used it when she had a lot of canning to do. I'd completely forgotten about it until I tripped over this fool trunk.

"Look," she continued, dragging Violet over to the contraption and flipping the lid open. "Before we head out to the field in the morning, we'll heat some meat and vegetables on the stove. Then we'll pour it into the stew pot, cover it up, close the lid, and it will keep cooking all day while we're gone. We'll have stew tomorrow night, Violet. A real meal!"

"No more eggs?" Violet regarded the hay box thoughtfully, assessing its possibilities, then threw her arms around Rachel in an exultant hug. "Then hooray for the hay box!"

❧

Rachel sat before the fire, her Bible open in her lap. Violet, reassured of Rachel's sanity, had gone off to bed. The squirrel, bedded down in the dynamite box with a splint on its injured leg, slept contentedly, and Rachel rejoiced in having some unaccustomed time to herself. She smoothed the pages with her hand, closing her eyes to reflect on the words from the Forty-sixth Psalm: "God is our refuge and strength, a very present help in trouble. Therefore will not we fear, though the earth be removed, and though the mountains be carried into the midst of the sea. . . ."

Rachel smiled drowsily, her soul at peace for the first time in weeks. God was with her, and she would not fear. Not even if Thumb Butte and Granite Mountain parted from their moorings and sailed away. Not even if Hiram Bradshaw showed his ugly, threatening face on her property. God was her help.

A tentative knock at the door interrupted her reverie, and she sprang up, shaking her head to clear it. Late night visits only meant trouble. She approached the door cautiously, one hand at her throat, trying to recapture the serenity she had felt only a moment before. Opening the door a mere crack, she peered out into the darkness.

"I'm sorry to call so late." The voice belonged to Daniel Moore. "I saw the light and figured you were still up. May I speak with you for a moment?"

Rachel frowned, then backed away, allowing him to enter the room. She stood near the fireplace, not offering him a seat. Whatever he had to say, he could say it quickly and be on his way. If he tried to give her any trouble, Pa's Henry rifle hung over the mantel less than an arm's length away.

&

"I've been thinking," Daniel said, unaffected by her lack of hospitality. "I can understand your reluctance to accept free help. I guess I'd feel the same way in your place. How about if we work it another way?"

"What did you have in mind?" Rachel asked, eyeing him suspiciously.

Daniel licked his lips, choosing his words with care. What could it be about this woman that turned his usual assurance into self-doubt? And why did she want to be so all-fired difficult? He only wanted to help. "What if I work for you, just like I offered the other night, but you pay me for it?" He raised his hand when she opened her mouth to protest.

"What I'm thinking is that *after* the loan payment is made, you and I split any profit that's left. That way, you'd be assured of making the payment, and you'd know I was giving you my best so there'd be as much profit as possible for us to share." He pasted a confident grin on his face that didn't at all match the uncertainty he felt.

Rachel measured him with calm brown eyes that seemed to probe his innermost being, and Daniel's heart beat faster. Finally, she nodded.

"It's a deal," she said solemnly, extending her hand to seal the bargain. "After the loan is paid, we'll split what's left right down the middle."

Daniel started to object that he'd figured on giving her and Violet the bigger share but clamped his lips shut and took her hand. She had agreed to let him help; he wouldn't jeopardize that by quibbling over the split. Her grip was firm, but not at all masculine. As little as he trusted women, he felt that when this one gave her word, a person could take that to the bank.

"I'll see you in the morning," he told her and let himself out.

❧

Rachel lay in her bed, looking up into the darkness. Had she done the right thing in striking a bargain with Daniel Moore? She truly believed God had shown her the way to save the farm by cutting out labor costs, but she now knew she and Violet could never do it alone.

Allowing Daniel to help should make it possible to save money like she'd planned, and paying him a percentage of what was left over would soothe her pride. There might not be much to divide between them, but that was a chance they would both take.

"You must have sent him, after all, Lord," she whispered

into the night. "Thank You for giving me a second chance. And thank You for reminding me about the hay box. You really are leading me one step at a time. . .even if some of those steps cause me to fall flat on my face!" She chuckled and rolled onto her side, drifting off to sleep.

❧

Rachel pulled the wagon to a stop behind Samson's General Store and smiled at Jake Samson when he came out the back door to help her unload. "Mornin', Rachel," he drawled, his genial face breaking into a mass of creases when he smiled. "What do you have today? I hope you brought more of those sweet carrots of yours."

"I have those, plus turnips, potatoes, and string beans." Rachel slid the sacks of vegetables down the wagon bed to Jake with a sense of satisfaction. Getting the harvest in on time might be a tricky proposition, but the vegetable business she and Pa had built up continued to flourish.

She pressed her lips together and took a deep breath. "I brought something else too," she said, trying to sound casual. "Would you be interested in some eggs?" She lifted the basket from its carefully padded resting place and held it out for Jake to see. The general store was her first stop today, and Jake had always been her favorite customer, but if he wasn't interested, she could always try the Prescott Mercantile and Grady's Market down the street.

Jake pursed his lips in a soundless whistle. "How'd you know folks have been clamoring for these?" He grinned and shook his head admiringly. "You're a shrewd one, all right, just like your pa. I'll pay you top dollar," he said, naming a price that took her breath away. "And I'll take every one you can bring, all right?"

Rachel finished her rounds in a happy daze. If the hens

kept laying like they had been, she calculated the eggs alone would bring in enough to keep them going from day to day, leaving the vegetable money free to go into the loan fund. Raising three hundred dollars by the fifteenth of December still seemed an unattainable goal, but God had been faithful to meet their needs so far. Surely He would open other opportunities to keep the farm safe.

Elated by her newfound source of income, she treated herself to a small bag of lemon drops and had nearly reached the wagon when a rough hand grabbed her by the elbow. Whirling, Rachel found herself staring at a faded checkered shirt front. She tilted her head back and looked up into close-set blue eyes that regarded her coldly.

"Hiram Bradshaw, what on earth do you think you're doing? Let go of me this minute." She twisted her arm to escape his grasp, but he only tightened his grip.

"We need to talk," he told her and propelled her unceremoniously past the corner of the market and into an alleyway between two buildings.

More angry than frightened, Rachel spun around to face him. "Are you out of your mind?" she demanded, wrenching her arm free at last. She glared at him while massaging her elbow where his meaty fingers had dug in. "I have nothing to say to you. Nothing at all."

Hiram's beefy face turned a dull red. "You'll have plenty to say to me before I'm through with you," he rasped. He took a step toward Rachel, his massive bulk looming over her, filling the narrow confines of the alley. Rachel backed away, her nose wrinkling in distaste at the smell of stale liquor on his breath.

"I hear you're having problems coming up with the money you owe on your farm. Looks like your pa wasn't the slick operator everyone thought he was." Hiram's mouth twisted in a crooked grin. "It's a shame he left you girls in such a fix."

"You need to find a better informant. We're doing fine, just fine." Rachel glowered at him, daring him to disagree. Now that Daniel was helping them, they'd be able to make the payment with no problem. She edged away, intending to slip between Hiram and the board-and-batten wall, but he propped an arm against the building to block her escape. Rachel backed away, feeling the rough-cut wood behind her snag the fabric of her dress.

Hiram continued as though she hadn't spoken. "There's no way you and your sister will be able to come up with that kind of money." He leaned closer, his heavy breath stirring the loose wisps of hair at the sides of her face. "I'd like to help you out. I'll give you a thousand for the place, and you two can move to town. No more breaking your pretty little back doing all that heavy work. What do you say?"

"I say you're just one step above a common thief!" Rachel retorted, eyes flashing. "You know as well as I do our place is worth at least three times that."

"It's a thousand more than you'll get when the bank forecloses. I'd hate to see you two sweet things out on the streets, penniless." He edged back, giving Rachel room to move again. "Think about it."

The cramped space barely gave her room to squeeze by him. She shrank back and slid past against the wall, preferring to risk a rip in her dress rather than any contact with Hiram. With his taunting voice echoing in her ears, she emerged from the alley and hurried to the wagon. "The nerve of that lout!" she fumed, heading the horses toward home.

Her earlier joy ebbed away, and an icy knot formed in her stomach. Was Hiram right? Could they really lose the farm? Despite his unappealing appearance and utter lack of manners,

Hiram had a reputation as a canny businessman. If he honestly thought they wouldn't be able to raise the money in time. . .

"Nonsense! The man just wants to get his grubby hands on our land, and I won't let it happen." They had Daniel's help now, and they would be all right. The faint suspicions she first felt when he'd offered to work for them returned, gnawing at her, teasing her with questions. Why would he want to spend so much time helping them, especially when he had no guarantee of much, if any, income for all his efforts? Did he have some unspoken motive?

Rachel fretted over those questions all the way home and had worked herself into a foul mood by the time she reached the house. Molly met her on the porch, wrapping around her ankles with loud purrs. Rachel looked at the cat, looked again, and stomped inside.

"Violet!" she hollered, glad to be able to vent her pent-up frustration.

Violet appeared in her bedroom doorway, cuddling her furry patient. "Look how much he's improved. He'll be ready to be on his own again in a few—"

"What have you been giving Molly?"

Cut off in midsentence, Violet stared, her face a puzzled blank. "What do you mean?"

"Don't play the innocent. I can tell you've been slipping her extra food." Rachel swung the door open and pointed dramatically. "Look at her. She's positively fat!"

"But Rachel, I—"

"It better not be eggs again. We're going to need every last one of them to sell in town. I appreciate your tender heart, Violet, but you need to realize we're going to have to tighten up until this land payment is taken care of." She leaned forward, jabbing a finger in the air to emphasize each word. "We'll have everything we can do just to feed ourselves. We certainly can't waste food on the cat."

Instead of looking contrite, Violet took a combative stance and raised her chin. "I don't know what she's been eating, but it didn't come from me, not after the way you got after me last time. We've been clearing the cornfield; maybe she's catching extra mice." With that, she tucked the squirrel back into his box and stalked off toward the kitchen garden.

Rachel stared after her, unconvinced, although she knew Violet was not a devious person. She tilted her head and considered Molly, now washing herself with slow, deliberate strokes of her tongue. "Extra mice, is it? You must have found every mouse in this part of Yavapai County." Molly stopped her cleaning and regarded Rachel coolly, then walked away in the direction of the barn, tail held high.

"You too?" Rachel muttered. She leaned back against the doorjamb, then slid down until she was sitting with her arms wrapped around her knees. First her sister, then the cat. Was everyone going to turn away from her?

She stared at the solid outline of Granite Mountain and shook her head slowly. Honesty compelled her to admit that Violet had ample justification for leaving in a huff. Even though she had a soft spot for animals and spoiled them rotten, she had never lied to Rachel. There had been no earthly reason to upbraid her like that.

Rachel buried her head in her arms. This whole miserable situation had turned her into a cynical shrew, suspicious of everyone. Although, she reminded herself, some people positively invited suspicion. "Like Hiram," she grumbled. "I wouldn't trust him as far as I could throw him."

"Do you always sit around in doorways talking to yourself?"

Rachel sat up with a start, cracking the back of her head on the doorjamb. Daniel stood at the bottom of the porch steps, one corner of his mouth tugging upward. Rachel scrambled to her feet. Being on the porch while he stood on the ground gave her the advantage of height, and she scowled at him from her superior position.

"Do you always sneak up on people like that?" she countered waspishly. "Seems like every time you come around, I wind up banging into something." She touched the back of her head gingerly, wincing when her fingers made contact with the sore spot.

Daniel's half smile immediately disappeared. "Are you bleeding?" he asked with concern and mounted the porch steps. "Let me look."

"I can take care of myself just fine, thank you," Rachel snapped. "Now what was it you wanted, besides scaring me half to death?" She fixed him with a steely glare, and the hand he had raised toward her dropped back to his side.

"I just wanted to let you know I'm ready to take another wagon load of corn over to Fort Whipple," he said stiffly.

"Oh. That's fine. I'll see you when you get back." Rachel stepped off the porch and strode away briskly, silently raking herself over the coals. Daniel had come to help them of his own free will, for goodness' sake. How long could she expect him to stay if she jumped down his throat every time he turned around? Her steps faltered, and she realized she had no idea where she was headed.

To the garden? No, Violet had gone there to get away from her. The barn was out too—even the cat didn't want to be near her. Rachel sighed and turned toward the cornfield. Out there, at least, she could do something productive.

❧

Daniel watched her walk away, easy grace in every stride. Why couldn't Ike have produced a quiet, easygoing daughter instead of this spitfire? On the other hand, a meek, docile woman wouldn't have the spirit needed to try to keep the place going. Rachel might be as prickly as the cactus that dotted the nearby hills, but he had to admit she wasn't afraid to get out and work hard. Most days she kept right up with him.

She didn't whine, either. He chuckled ruefully, remembering the way she'd lit into him, even though her head must have hurt like anything after that whack she gave it. He admired that kind of grit and determination, and she'd need every bit of it if she truly planned to make a go of this place.

He stared after Rachel's retreating figure, growing smaller in the distance. When he'd made the offer to help out, he wasn't sure whether she'd accept or throw him off the place. He was beginning to be glad she had taken him up on it. She might not be a delicate beauty like her sister, but she was one very intriguing woman, this Rachel Canfield.

four

Rachel gave the clothes in the washtub a final stir, then straightened, pressing her fingers into the small of her back. She swiped at the dampness on her forehead with the back of her wrist and shook her head wearily. This time of year, a body expected crisp fall weather, not temperatures nearly as warm as summertime.

She rolled up her sleeves and set the washboard in place, preparing to give their clothes a good scrubbing. It galled her to lose the time she should be spending in the field to this chore, but it couldn't be helped. She ignored the laundry as long as she could, and the only relatively clean clothes she and Violet owned consisted of the ones they stood up in. Violet generously offered to do the wash, but they both knew she didn't have the stamina to carry out the strenuous chore. Rachel set her to mending instead.

No wonder Pa left the farm solely to Rachel. He knew that, try as she might, Violet would never have the staying power needed for the outdoor work. Even the heavier indoor chores sometimes taxed her delicate strength.

Over a year ago, Pa shared his misgivings with Rachel when she took him a cold drink in the field one midsummer morning. "I may have made a mistake bringing your sister out here," he'd said, rubbing his hand across his forehead the way he did when a decision faced him and he couldn't make up his mind. "The way things were back in Missouri, it seemed like the right thing to do."

He tilted his hat back and mopped his lined forehead, squinting at the cloudless summer sky. "Even with the war being over for more than a decade, folks still held so much hatred and bitterness in their hearts. Fellas would have come crowding around you girls one day, and I didn't like the looks of any I saw. Didn't know if I could trust a one of them. Out here," his gesture encompassed a region far broader than the farm they'd carved from the forest, "it didn't matter so much which side a man had fought on. Politics didn't amount to much. What counted was what he'd made of himself since then. I wanted you two to have a real choice when the time came. When the fever came and took your ma, I figured it was a good time to move on and make a new start."

Rachel nodded soberly, remembering the dark days of her mother's death. "You were right to do it, Pa." The words came out in a whisper. "Coming out here helped us all."

He flashed her a quick smile of gratitude before his face grew thoughtful again. "I'm not so sure about Violet. She's frail, like your mother. I should have seen that in her before we left home, I guess, but I thought she'd grow strong out here." He shook his head slowly. "When it comes time for her to think about a husband, we'll have to make sure she gets the right one. She's going to need a town man, Rachel. Violet isn't like you; she'll never make a farm wife." His eyes lit up again, and he looked at his older daughter with pride.

Rachel relived that moment, remembering how proud she'd been of his accolade. Looking around her now at the tub of clothes still awaiting her attention, the corn yet unharvested in the field, and the kitchen garden in need of weeding, her heart sank. What would he think now, to see the myriad chores still left undone? She closed her eyes, ready to admit defeat, then she raised her chin and squared her shoulders. Pa had believed in her. Somehow she'd find the strength to make a go of the place he'd worked so hard to build. She wouldn't let him down.

She reached for the washboard once more, then paused when she noticed the buggy out on the road. She puffed out an impatient sigh. With all the work ahead of her today, she just didn't have time for company. She watched the buggy, hoping it would pass by and continue on toward Jeb McCurdy's. Instead, it slowed and turned in to her place.

Rachel smoothed back the strands of hair that had fallen loose from her bun and pasted on a smile. Maybe she could get rid of whoever it was before they wasted too much of her time. With the sun in her eyes, she couldn't see more than just a silhouette stepping down and walking toward her. She shaded her eyes with her hand, and the smile froze on her face when she recognized Hiram Bradshaw.

"What are you doing out here?" she demanded, dropping all pretense at a cordial welcome.

Unabashed, Hiram strode toward her like he owned the place already, stopping only a foot away from where she stood. His bold gaze moved over her from head to toe and back again, and his knowing smirk made gooseflesh prickle all up and down Rachel's arms. If Daniel had been around, she would have hollered for him, pride or no pride, but he had left earlier to make another delivery to Fort Whipple.

With an uneasy glance toward the house, she considered her options. A cry of alarm would bring Violet outside in a hurry, but she couldn't bring herself to subject her gentle sister to Hiram's ugly leer. She would just have to brazen it out and get rid of the man as soon as she possibly could.

Hiram rocked back on his heels and regarded her thoughtfully. "You're looking right pretty today, Rachel. A trifle tired, maybe, but pretty, all the same."

Rachel stood her ground, determined not to give way before his insolent stare. She lifted her chin. "I asked you what you were doing here."

"Not very friendly today, are you?" Hiram's thin lips drew back in a grin. "I had some business out this way, so I decided to stop by and visit a bit." He studied the house and the out-buildings. "I'd forgotten just how nice a setup you have here. Old Ike knew how to do well for himself, and that's a fact."

"I don't have time for small talk," Rachel told him, trying to keep her voice steady. "I have chores to do, so if you'll excuse me. . ."

Hiram didn't take the hint. He stood squarely in front of the washtub, just where Rachel needed to be. She crossed her arms to give herself some measure of comfort. She could no more force herself to move that close to Hiram than she could pet a rattlesnake. Well, if he felt inclined to take up space there, she had a hundred other things to do. Without a word, she spun on her heel and set off in the direction of the barn with Hiram dogging her heels.

Rachel fumed and blinked back angry tears. He had no right to be there, none at all. If it hadn't been for his inflexible position on their loan, she and Violet wouldn't be working like slaves trying to bring the harvest in with only Daniel's help.

His presence only intensified the desperation that gnawed at her night and day. If she had the strength to throw the man off her property by brute force, she would. Failing that, she would just have to maintain her composure and wait until he tired of his game of cat and mouse and decided to leave.

Whatever she did, she mustn't show fear. That would only serve to fuel the flames of Hiram's bullying ways. A demeanor impervious to his provocative jibes was her only hope of protection.

In the barn, she forked hay to the milk cow, all the while keeping a wary eye on Hiram, who leaned against the center post, content to watch her work. Rachel couldn't help but compare his behavior with Daniel's. Daniel didn't try to stop her from working alongside him—*as if he could!* she told herself with a sniff—but he would never stand by and watch her labor alone.

A jumble of garden tools lay heaped in a corner near the wide door. Violet had neglected to return them to their proper places, she thought, pursing her lips in irritation. Not a surprising discovery, but definitely an annoyance. She bent to set the implements in some sort of order. Straightening up the hoes and shovels didn't rank very high on her growing list of things to do, but it did have the advantage of keeping her busy and able to ignore Hiram.

She picked up a three-pronged pitchfork. How did this one come to be in the pile with the tools from outside? It belonged up in the loft, ready to pitch hay down for the horses and cow. Rachel hefted it in one hand, hesitating at the thought of putting herself in a vulnerable position on the ladder or being cornered in the loft by Hiram.

Then she eyed the fork's sharp tines and grinned. She wouldn't be all that vulnerable. It would serve him right to be on the receiving end of the keen-edged points. She mounted the ladder rungs and climbed upward, almost hoping he'd try something.

Instead of pursuing her, Hiram began circling the interior of the barn, thumping the walls and trying to shake the uprights.

"Good and solid," he said with an approving smirk. "Nice to see it won't need much work."

Rachel clamped her lips together and resisted the impulse

to fling the pitchfork straight at him. She could always say she'd dropped it. She clambered back down, picked up the egg basket, and strode out the door toward the chicken coop. Normally, Violet took charge of the chickens, but the chore gave Rachel the opportunity to keep occupied and keep moving. . .away from Hiram.

If only Daniel would come! He could set her free from her dilemma in short order. Her steps faltered when she realized the direction her thoughts had taken. When had she started looking to Daniel for protection? His only purpose in helping them was to repay the debt he felt he owed their father, nothing more. She couldn't get used to the idea of having him around for long. He'd be gone as soon as the harvest ended.

But the only reason she wanted him here today, her mind argued, was to get rid of Hiram. That didn't mean she wished to pursue a more personal relationship with him, just that it would be nice to have some masculine strength available when she needed it. The kind of protection she'd always taken for granted when Pa was around. She didn't need or want Daniel for anything more than that.

No point in dwelling on such thoughts in any case, she thought drearily. Daniel wouldn't be coming back any time soon.

"How's the harvest coming?"

Lost in her thoughts, Rachel started at the grating sound of Hiram's voice. "Fine," she snapped and resumed her brisk strides toward the chicken coop. "You can see for yourself." She nodded toward the cornfields off to her left where over half the crop had already been cut and delivered.

Much to her relief, Hiram stopped and stood gazing across the land. With a renewed sense of freedom, she hurried to the coop. She set the basket down and used an old can to scoop cracked corn into her gathered apron. The hens followed her to the end of the chicken yard, clucking in anticipation, then diving after the yellow morsels when she scattered them on the ground.

Rachel watched them bob their heads and peck at the kernels. "Eat hearty," she told them. "You need to get lots of food so you can lay lots of eggs. You're going to help me save the farm." She stood a moment, smiling at their awkward antics. How long had it been since she'd taken the time to do anything more than run from one chore to the next?

She shifted her gaze from the greedy birds to the hills around her. Their short-lived summer greenery had disappeared, to be replaced by the tawny tones of autumn. The fawn-colored grasses made a pleasing contrast with the muted green of the juniper trees. Rachel heaved a weary sigh. It seemed like ages since she'd had even a moment to appreciate the beauty of her surroundings, but she and Pa used to take time to enjoy the splendor of God's creation regularly.

She and Pa. The pain of his absence hit her afresh like the stab of a knife. They wouldn't share any more times of wonder together, at least not this side of heaven. She gave her apron a final shake and went back to collect her basket. She would collect the eggs while the hens were off the nest and occupied with their food. Surely seeing all that potential income and thinking of the promise of more to come would help boost her spirits.

It took a moment for her eyes to adjust to the dimness of the coop's interior. The comforting smells of earth and straw filled her nostrils, bringing a renewed sense of well-being. With her every waking moment spent trying to find ways to stretch their meager funds, she had almost forgotten how much she enjoyed working with the animals. Their easy contentment served as a lesson in taking life as it came and not fretting over what might lie ahead.

Once her eyes had adapted to the change in light, she scanned the nests and lifted the precious eggs into her basket one by one. Soft clucking sounds came from behind the corn bin, and she dropped to her knees to investigate. One of the hens huddled on a makeshift nest, watching Rachel with a baleful eye. Rachel clicked her tongue. Violet must have missed those eggs, and the biddy had decided to settle on the nest to hatch them.

Rachel reconsidered her initial indignation at the loss of income from those eggs. They had a steady supply now. It wouldn't hurt to have a new batch of hens coming up as replacement layers for the year ahead. She started to rise but stopped when she spotted an egg resting in a dark corner, then another. Finding every single egg could be something of a challenge, she admitted, reaching far beneath the roosts to extract the last one.

She wrinkled her nose at its dusty appearance. Evidently Violet had missed it too, and for quite some time by the looks of it. She set it gingerly atop the pile, planning to bury it before she took the rest of her booty into the house.

Grabbing the lid of the corn bin to help pull herself to her feet, she heard the door thump softly. "Thought I'd lost you." Hiram's voice came from directly behind her. She whirled, her heart pounding. How could she have forgotten his unwanted presence?

"Looks like you've been keeping right on top of things around here," he conceded. "Must be awful hard for a couple of women alone to deal with, though. You really need a man around here to keep the place going." He narrowed the gap between them to mere inches with one step.

Rachel felt her throat tighten. She tried to step back, but her shoulders collided with the wall. "It's time you left, Hiram," she said, trying not to let her alarm show in her voice.

"Remember the offer I made you the other day?" He leaned closer, as if she hadn't spoken. "I have another one." He lifted his hand and traced her jawline with a fleshy thumb.

Rachel shrank back against the rough boards, feeling the sharp splinters dig into her shoulder blades. With sickening clarity, she realized all too well the limitations of the coop's confined space.

Hiram's cold blue gaze bored into hers. He edged closer still. "You could keep the farm, Rachel. . .as my wife."

Her mouth fell open. "Your wi—" she began, but bile rose into her constricted throat, and she couldn't continue. Disgust and panic lent her strength, and she twisted sharply to one side. The move increased the distance between them but put Hiram between her and the door.

She tried to ignore the metallic taste in her mouth and ordered her heaving stomach to settle down. "Get out," she rasped, forcing each word through stiff lips. "This farm is not for sale. . . and neither am I." She took one step back, still clutching the egg basket.

five

Hiram's hand flashed out and seized her arm in a pincer grip. Panic threatened to blind her. With a wild cry, she wrenched her arm free from Hiram's grasp, steadying the teetering basket. Her hand closed on the first egg she touched, and she hurled it at Hiram with all her strength.

The egg splattered across Hiram's face, and a putrid stench exploded through the coop. Rachel gagged and pulled the skirt of her apron over her nose and mouth. Through watering eyes, she could see Hiram bent double, raking at the slimy mess. Taking advantage of his distraction, she pushed past him and made her escape.

Away from the reek of the sulfurous fumes, she filled her lungs with sweet, clean air again and again. The door slammed open, and Hiram emerged, his face suffused with fury.

"You!" he snarled and started toward her.

"Not another step," she ordered. Of its own accord, her hand held up another egg, poised for throwing. She almost laughed out loud when Hiram froze in his tracks. "I told you you weren't welcome here. Maybe now you'll believe me. Now get!" She took several steps backward, then wheeled around and hurried toward the house, straining her ears to pick up any sound of pursuit.

"I'm going to enjoy seeing you hauled out of here kicking and screaming," he bellowed. "I'll be standing right here when they drag you and your sister off this farm. Have you thought about what you'll do to keep body and soul together

47

when you lose the place? Life isn't easy for a woman alone. It isn't always kind, either. You remember that!"

Rachel reached the safety of the porch and let herself inside the house, closing the door on his angry threats. She eased back the edge of the curtain with her finger and watched Hiram stomp off to his buggy. With an angry crack of his whip, he lashed his horse and drove the buggy out onto the road to town.

And out of her life, she hoped, although she doubted her circumstances warranted such optimism. She leaned back against the door, fighting the urge to slide to the floor and bury her face in shaking hands. Hiram's rage had unsettled her more than she cared to admit.

Pitching the rotten egg at him had been the only way she knew to defend herself at the time, but it had also cut off any hope that Hiram might be swayed by pleas of leniency. If she couldn't raise the money for the loan payment in time, she knew he would show no mercy.

But she couldn't allow herself to dwell on that dismal prospect. Sinking into a mire of such gloomy thoughts would only send her spirits spiraling into despair. Wallowing in melancholy might be tempting, but it wouldn't get the work done. With a groan, she pushed herself upright and walked toward the kitchen, where she could hear the clanking of pots and pans. Violet must be starting supper.

Her sister looked up when she stopped in the doorway. "Was that Hiram Bradshaw?" she asked. "What got him all stirred up?" Her nose wrinkled, and her eyes grew round. "Rachel, what on earth is that awful stench? You didn't run into a skunk, did you?" Her gaze dropped to Rachel's hands and her lips formed an *O*. "Did you get hold of a bad egg?"

Rachel glanced down and saw she still held the basket. A

basket only half full. She had lost more than the one she threw at Hiram in her dash for freedom.

Violet's forehead crinkled in concern. "You didn't have to do my chores, Rachel. I meant to tend to the chickens right after I fixed us something to eat."

"It's all right. I didn't think you'd neglected them. I just needed something to do right then, so I took care of them for you." She turned and hurried to her room before Violet could ask why she'd needed something more to occupy her on an already busy day. Violet didn't need to know the details of Hiram's visit. . .or hear any hint of his proposal.

In the privacy of her room, Rachel filled the bathtub with water she'd intended for the laundry, glad she didn't have to wait for it to heat. She started to unbutton her dress, then stopped in dismay. Until she finished the wash, she didn't have another clean garment to her name. What on earth could she do? All Violet's dresses soaked in the tub along with her own, and they were at least two sizes too small for her, anyway.

She tiptoed out to the cupboard where some of Pa's clothes were still kept. Silly, she guessed, but she hadn't had the heart to dispose of all of them yet. She pulled a shirt and a pair of overalls from a drawer and eyed them doubtfully. They would have to do, she decided. She only needed to wear them until her own clothes were clean and dry once more. Surely there wouldn't be any more visitors today.

With her mind made up, she carried them back to her room, pulled off her dress and underthings, and stepped into the tub.

Rachel closed her eyes, savoring the warmth of the steaming water. She reached for the soap and began to scrub, wishing she could scour away the memory of Hiram's nearness as easily as the smell of rotten egg. She pulled a strand of hair loose and sniffed. *Phew!* She would have to wash it too.

Even after her skin glowed pink and her hair hung over her shoulders in a damp cascade, Rachel stayed in the tub, longing to close her eyes again and relax just a few moments. It took all the force of will she possessed to get to her feet and begin toweling herself dry. Chores still awaited her, piled up even higher now that she'd lost so much time due to Hiram's visit and its aftermath. She squeezed the water out of her hair and thought bleakly of the days ahead.

Would the work ever ease up? She spent every waking moment tending to some aspect of the farm, whether working in the field or the garden, delivering vegetables and eggs to town, or totting up the latest figures in her ledger.

Even in her sleep, the constant worry never completely left her. More than once, she had awakened with a start after a series of nightmares. The worst one returned to haunt her again and again. In it, she and Violet stood on the porch in the dim light of a cold, gray dawn. Each of them held a small bag containing two dresses and a nightshirt. All their other belongings, even the photographs of Ma and Pa, had to stay behind. Weeping piteously, the girls clutched one another, knowing they were about to leave their home, never to return.

A grim-faced sheriff stood at the foot of the porch steps, ready to remove them by force if need be. Even their most heartrending appeals failed to move him. He never changed expression, only pointed toward the road with an unyielding arm. Feeling as though she were stepping off the edge of an abyss, Rachel put her arm around Violet's shoulders and led her off the porch. At the same moment, snow began to fall, huge flakes that tumbled from the sky and blotted out the distant landscape.

Blinking to see through the heavy flurry, Rachel could make out only one object: Hiram Bradshaw stood at the edge of their property, thumbs hooked behind his belt, and his mouth wide open in a triumphant laugh.

At that point she would sit bolt upright, chest heaving and covered with droplets of sweat despite the chill of the autumn night. Smoothing out the tangled sheets and blotting the tears from her face brought back some sense of normalcy, but she found it took longer each time to convince herself the unnerving experience had only been a dream.

Then there were the household duties. Using the hay box had freed both her and Violet from having to spend hours over the stove, but the remaining kitchen chores demanded attention, all the same. Violet took care of most of those as well as tending to the animals, but her gentle, dreamy sister was too easily diverted by any distraction that happened to catch her attention to always keep her mind on the task at hand. Thus, Rachel had to add keeping tabs on Violet to her other responsibilities.

She pulled Pa's shirt on over her head and stepped into the overalls, feeling burdened beyond her ability to cope. His clothes hung on her, and she leaned over to roll up the legs. Her fingers traced over a spot she'd mended for him just last spring. When Pa was alive, they'd worked plenty hard, but they still found time at the end of the day to visit and share with one another. Time to discuss the day's events, to reminisce about the past and plan for the future. Rachel worked her brush through the wet tangles in her hair and felt the hot sting of tears behind her eyelids.

What would she and Violet do if she didn't come up with the cash they needed by December 15? Hiram's dark allusions to the possible fate of penniless young women alone in the world haunted her. She had heard enough about other destitute girls forced to earn their keep in the saloons along Whiskey Row to know there was some truth to his assertions. Bad enough to think about letting Pa down by losing the farm; how could she bear it if she put Violet in peril of some hideous fate?

The sun moved further along its circuit through the sky, and still Rachel sat on the edge of her bed, staring into the prospects of a dismal future. How could they have reached such desperate straits in so short a time?

All she had ever wanted was to help Pa on the farm and someday to marry a hardworking farmer like him. Never had she faced the prospect of having to contemplate a different sort of existence. Farm life was all she cared about, all she ever wanted. She bent over and covered her face with her hands. Pa had admonished her about her stubborn streak more than once. Had she been so bent on following her own desires that she had never considered the possibility that God might have something quite different in mind for her?

A new thought struck her with the force of a blow. Just how much did staying here mean to her? Would she ever be so desperate to cling to her beloved farm that she'd entertain the notion of accepting Hiram's offer, or one like it? She shuddered, not knowing whether she felt more repulsed by his contemptible proposition or herself for giving the idea even a fleeting consideration. She would find some way to keep body and soul together without compromising their honor. She had to.

She started to pull back her damp hair, then shrugged and decided to leave it hanging loose. With all the work still left to be done before dark, she couldn't spare even the few seconds it would take to twist it into a bun. Besides, it would dry more quickly that way. She picked up her reeking dress and carried it out her door at arm's length, so intent on getting back to her washing that she nearly crashed into Violet.

"Rachel, have you seen Molly?"

"Not lately," she said, debating whether to heat fresh water or use what she already had. She didn't know how clean the clothes would be if she didn't take the time to reheat it, but maybe soaking as long as they had already would be enough. She stepped onto the porch and glanced at the sun. The water they'd been sitting in would have to suffice, she decided. She just didn't have enough time to start over.

Violet touched her arm. "Rachel?"

"At least they'll be cleaner than they were, and that's a mercy."

"Rachel!" Violet's urgent tone finally claimed her attention.

"What is it?" she demanded.

Violet's lower lip quivered at the brusque question, but she continued. "I said I can't find Molly anywhere. Could you help me look?"

Giving her sister an exasperated glance, Rachel went down the steps and reached into the tepid water, grabbing the first garment her hands touched. She set the washboard into position and scrubbed the dress back and forth across its rough ridges.

Violet followed and took a challenging stance, hands on her hips. "You could at least answer me. I'm worried about her."

"I don't have time," Rachel replied, nettled by the new interruption. "With everything else that needs to be done, I really can't get too worked up about a cat." She clenched her teeth together before she could say more, not wanting to snap at her sister.

"She's not just any cat. She's Molly! I thought you cared

about her." Violet whirled and went out to resume her search, but not before Rachel noted the crystal droplets shimmering on her lashes. She sighed in annoyance. How could Violet be concerned over something so foolish when real problems stared them in the face?

She worked her way through the clothes, fuming about her sister's behavior. If Violet would pay more attention to her responsibilities and spend less time fretting about nonsensical things like missing cats, maybe Rachel wouldn't have to shoulder the burden of their predicament alone.

Looking down at the water running from her elbows to the legs of Pa's overalls, a grimace of wry amusement twisted her lips. At least one good thing had come out of Violet's preoccupation with the cat's whereabouts. She'd been so worked up about Molly that she hadn't even noticed Rachel's unusual garb.

six

Daniel shifted on the wagon seat and tipped his hat brim down to shield his eyes from the sun. He hadn't planned on getting back this late, but the long conversation over coffee in the supply sergeant's quarters had been a profitable one.

The sergeant's usually cheerful demeanor had been shadowed by worry over the low supply of fodder for the cavalry horses. When Daniel casually mentioned the enormous pile of cornstalks back at the farm, the soldier slapped his hand on the table and pledged to buy them all.

The extra money would be a welcome addition to their income. It had been time well spent.

Once he'd taken care of the horses, he'd be more than ready to tuck into a hot meal. He chuckled, wondering what Rachel and Violet had decided to fix for supper. He'd eaten better since he started working on the Canfield place than he had in months. No doubt about it, baching had its disadvantages, and one of them was having to put up with his own cooking.

The horses swung into the turnoff of their own accord and plodded toward the barn. Daniel squinted into the sun, trying to make out the forms in front of the house. A lone figure bent over the washtub. Daniel frowned. Rachel had told him she planned to use the day for household chores, but he would have thought the wash would have been finished long before this.

Had she hired someone to come in and help? He didn't

recognize the overall-clad fellow. Wait. He slitted his eyes and stared in disbelief. A man with long brown hair? He blinked and took a second look, then let out a hearty guffaw when he identified the stranger as Rachel.

She raised her head and glared at him. Daniel wiped the smile from his face. What other woman did he know who would wear such outrageous garb? But then, he never quite knew what to expect from Rachel Canfield. She could work as hard outdoors as a man and still fix some of the lightest biscuits he'd ever tasted. The woman was a surprising blend of grit and femininity, and all the more captivating for her unpredictability.

"Looks like your pa's shirt fits you better than it did me," he said, unable to resist the urge to tease her. A rosy blush crept from below the shirt collar to tint her face and neck.

"It's about time you got back," she snapped. "What did you do, decide to take the long way home?"

Daniel only grinned. With that tinge of pink staining her cheeks and her hair hanging loose to her waist, she looked like a petulant little girl, but he wasn't about to tell her so. In her present testy mood, she'd probably heave a bucket of that wash water all over him.

"I got some good news at the fort," he told her, outlining his deal to sell cornstalks to the soldiers. "It will mean a few more trips over there, but it'll be more than worth it."

"Oh." Rachel's expression softened a trifle. She twisted the apron she held to wring out the rinse water and marched up the steps to hang it over the porch railing.

Daniel watched her hair swing behind her, his gaze following its rippling motion in fascination. *Almost looks like a mountain waterfall.* He'd seen shady forest pools just that color of oak-leaf brown.

He caught himself up with a start. Where had those thoughts come from? Calling himself all kinds of a fool, he clicked his tongue at the horses and urged them toward the barn once more.

☙

Rachel shook out another of Violet's dresses and hung it up to dry. With such a late start, the clothes would probably have to stay out all night. She kept on draping the rest of the laundry over the porch rail and the rope Pa had strung at one side of the house, one part of her mind on the job at hand, the other intent on watching the barn door.

Funny how things never turned out quite the way you'd expect. She should have been mortified when Daniel came upon her wearing Pa's clothes. But instead of being shocked, he'd sounded amused, and much to Rachel's surprise, his teasing comment had put her at ease.

Daniel's look had been nothing like Hiram's. She'd seen nothing improper in his gaze, only acceptance of an unexpected situation. Pa would have done much the same thing, she thought, a small smile curving her lips. He wouldn't have questioned why she had chosen such an outlandish getup, only assumed that she must have had a good reason.

It felt good to have that kind of unquestioning approval again. She hadn't realized just how much she'd missed it. Some of her weariness lifted, and her shoulders straightened as though a physical weight had been lifted.

Daniel emerged from the barn and started to swing the heavy doors closed. Good. If he'd agree to take over feeding the animals and shutting them up for the night, her chores could be finished before supper. Her smile faded when she saw Violet approach Daniel, laying a pleading hand on his arm.

Violet and her cat! Fortunately, Daniel understood the

need to ignore such foolishness and focus on important matters. Her mouth fell open when he patted Violet on the shoulder and set off with her, apparently in search of Molly.

Rachel gritted her teeth. This was too much. She would have to take Violet to task about it later, after Daniel left. So much for any expectation of his help. She flung the last garment across the line and prepared to finish the chores herself.

Daniel walked into the barn just as she climbed down from the loft after forking down the last ration of hay for the day. "About ready for supper?" he asked.

"Did you find Molly?" she asked in a tone that rivaled a November frost.

"No. Violet's plenty worried about her too."

Rachel whirled on him. "Maybe Violet should try worrying about keeping this place going, instead of wasting her time on a fool cat. I could use more help around here."

"Whoa." Daniel held up his hand and regarded her thoughtfully. "Who are you really talking about here, Violet or me?"

Rachel drew in deep gulps of air. She knew if she opened her mouth again she couldn't control the tremor in her voice, knew she felt her frustration so keenly she might not be able to stop the flow of angry words once she got started. She pressed her lips together, but they tumbled out in spite of her efforts.

"How could you run off and spend the time on a fool's errand like that when there's so much work to be done? Violet should have better sense than to ask you to do something so trifling when you were late getting back in the first place. . . and you should have known better than to indulge her like that."

Daniel's sandy eyebrows drew together. "Have you looked at your sister lately? Really looked at her? She's hurting, Rachel. Remember, she lost her father too. Maybe she needs a bit more babying than she's been getting. Frankly, I'm a lot more concerned about Violet than the cat."

The truth of his words hit home like an arrow finding its mark. Rachel braced her feet and lifted her chin to keep him from seeing how his accusation had staggered her. "You'd better wash up," she told him through stiff lips. "It's time for supper."

He stared at his feet a moment, then lifted his gaze to meet hers. "Not tonight. I'll be heading on home. I have some chores of my own to do, and I don't want to be late in the morning."

He turned on his heel and left. Rachel stood rooted to the spot until he had ridden out and disappeared down the road. Even with both hands clamped across her mouth, she was unable to stifle the whimper that rose in her throat. How much would her stubborn pride cost her before she learned to control her tongue?

ε&

How could anyone so outwardly appealing manage to turn into a snarling wildcat at the least provocation? Daniel turned the question over in his mind on the way back to his diggings. The new source of income he'd discovered that day meant financial help not only for this season but for the years ahead. The Canfields' situation had taken a major turn for the better, yet Rachel seemed bent on finding something to raise a fuss about, no matter how much their outlook improved.

And what about that business of him being late? If he hadn't spent the extra time with the supply sergeant, he never would have learned of their need for stalks that would have otherwise gone to waste. It just went to show you could never tell about women. The way he felt right now, he'd be happy if he never saw Miss Rachel Canfield again. Still, there was his debt to Ike, and he didn't take his obligations lightly.

seven

After a night's sleep, Daniel looked on the previous day's encounter from a new perspective. He'd been so elated by his business deal, then so troubled about Violet that he had failed to take into consideration the extreme pressure Rachel was under.

He knew how the nearing deadline weighed upon her, but instead of easing her burden, he had only added to it. Remorse for his shortsightedness gnawed at him. Hadn't he seen grown men snap with little more provocation than Rachel had experienced over the past months? She needed some relief and needed it fast.

Daniel mulled over the possibilities while he grabbed a quick breakfast and went about his morning chores. Washing up his dishes took only a few moments, and he didn't have much else to do around his temporary dwelling. Rachel had never inquired where he lived, and he wasn't about to tell her he'd thrown together this little hut just up the road from them in a matter of days once she agreed to let him stay and help out. Knowing her reluctance to accept his aid in the first place, he could just imagine what her reaction to that would have been.

There had to be some way to lighten the millstone around Rachel's neck, he thought while tossing a worn quilt over his cot. He couldn't guarantee it, but it looked to him like she should have enough to pay her debt to the bank on time. Rachel wouldn't rest, though, until she held the money in her hand.

He hung the washed pot back over the cold fire and prepared to leave for the day, chuckling at his quickly erected shelter. If Rachel got a glimpse of it, she would never believe he'd taken enough from his mining claim over the past two years to build up a sizable nest egg. More than enough to pay off her loan, in fact.

Why not do just that? He mounted his horse and set off, excitement rising in him at the thought. He could give Rachel the full amount, let her pay him off without a fixed deadline, and she could settle up with him whenever she had the funds to do so. It would solve everything. He tried to picture Rachel's reaction when he sprang the idea on her, and his enthusiasm crumbled into dust.

He knew full well what her reaction to such a gesture would be. Rachel, with her stubborn pride, would work until she dropped rather than take on another loan.

Scowling, he refused to admit his idea had run into a dead end. True, Rachel had a feisty, independent nature, but she was a hard worker, honest, and fiercely loyal. The type of woman a man could trust, if such a creature existed. Somehow Daniel knew he'd want to help Rachel out of this fix, even if he'd never met Ike Canfield.

He turned his horse into the corral and carried his tack into the barn. A flash of color caught his attention, and he spied Violet poking around in the dark recesses of an empty stall.

"Hasn't Molly turned up yet?"

The young girl turned at the sound of his voice, giving him the full effect of her startlingly blue eyes. With that lustrous dark hair and her heart-shaped face, she'd be downright beautiful one of these days, he thought. Rachel would have her hands full trying to keep hopeful suitors at bay once they noticed her.

"I don't know where else to look," she said. Her eyes brimmed with tears. "I can't find her anywhere. Do you think something's happened to her?"

A lot of things could have happened, but Daniel wasn't going to tell her that. Not right now, at least. Life in Arizona Territory wasn't easy for rugged men, let alone a small animal like Molly. She could easily have been picked off by an owl, or fallen prey to a pack of coyotes, or met one of any number of brutal ends. "Hard to say," he told her and left it at that.

Her frail shoulders slumped. "I guess I'd better get back to my chores. Rachel said she'll get me if she catches me lolly-gagging again."

Daniel stared after her. Something about Violet brought out a protective streak he hadn't known he possessed. *Would having a little sister or a daughter be anything like this?* He scoffed at his fancy, wondering where that errant thought had come from.

Turning to hang up his bridle, he stopped in midstride when a thought gripped him. When he first showed up with his offer of help, Rachel had turned him down flat. Not until he balanced out the proposition by adding some benefit to himself had she been willing to consent. He now faced the same sort of situation. Rachel would never accept an outright advance of money, but what if he made one modification to his bargain? What if he asked Rachel to marry him?

The more he thought about it, the more enthusiastic he became. He would present the plan as honestly as he knew how, letting Rachel know right up front that he offered it as a business proposition rather than a romantic proposal. She valued straight talk; she would appreciate his forthrightness.

He went over the advantages so they'd be straight in his mind when he talked to her. With him on the scene, Rachel would never need to worry again about having to run the farm on her own. And as his wife, she should have no objection to him making the land payment for her. For himself, he'd once again have a place to belong after years on his own and someone to talk to after a long day's work. Meeting Violet's needs as well would be almost like having a daughter, and with him around, he thought with a chuckle, Rachel would have much-needed help in dealing with her sister's would-be beaus.

Daniel slapped his hands on his knees, delighted with his plan. As a practical solution for them both, he didn't see how anyone could improve on it. He would be giving up some of his independence, true, but during the times the farm work slacked off he would still be able to spend time at his mining claim. Plenty of other men did that, and they got along just fine, so marriage shouldn't cramp his freedom too much.

Sometimes life called for a man to make a noble gesture for a good cause, and he felt pleased to be able to rise to the occasion. Now he only had to present the scheme to Rachel. He went off toward the cornfield, rehearsing what he would say in his mind to make sure he had the words right when he approached her.

&

Rachel shook the dirt from the bunch of carrots in her hand and stuffed them into her gunnysack. She could see Daniel swinging the corn knife, its blade flashing in the sun. *Thank goodness.* After yesterday's blowup, she couldn't have blamed him if he'd decided never to come around again.

She sat back on her heels and watched him wrap a length of twine around another shock. As far as she could see, he was putting as much energy into his work as ever, maybe even more. How nice to know he didn't hold a grudge!

She had prayed for forgiveness for her attitude the night before and made her peace with Violet over breakfast. She would have to make amends with Daniel at the first opportunity. After all, she had asked the Lord for help, and He'd sent it. She couldn't expect Him to shower her with further blessings if she didn't show appreciation for what He'd already given.

Some of her tension dropped away, and her mouth curved in a small smile. Daniel knew how to work hard, almost as if he loved the land as much as she did.

When the sun reached its zenith, she hurried back to the house to clean up before Daniel came in for lunch. She wanted to be presentable when she made her apology. To her surprise, he had already finished washing up before she arrived.

His freshly washed hands and face and slicked-back hair told her he'd taken some pains with his appearance. She hesitated, wondering if she should speak to him in her present grubby state, then decided to hurry to her room for a few quick moments with her washbasin and hairbrush. Then she would have the confidence to face him.

"Just a minute," Daniel called when she started to step through the doorway. "I'd like to talk to you, if you don't mind."

Rachel looked down at her dusty clothes and made a wry face. Did the Lord want to give her a lesson in humility as well as gratitude? "All right," she sighed.

Daniel led her a short distance away from the house. "I'd rather Violet didn't overhear us," he explained.

That suited Rachel. Admitting she'd been wrong didn't come easily for her. She would just as soon have no witnesses. She looked at Daniel, enjoying the way the sunlight glinted in his hair. His deep green eyes held only sincerity, and their frank expression twisted at her heart. The man had offered his aid to two strangers in their time of need. He had shown them nothing but decency and a willingness to help. How on earth could she have spoken to him the way she did?

"I needed to talk to you too," she began.

"All right. Just hear me out first," Daniel put in.

Rachel felt a twinge of impatience. Wasn't it just like a man to insist on getting his word in first when she was trying to apologize? "What I have to say won't take long."

"Neither will this."

"But listen—"

"I think we ought to get married."

Rachel froze, aware that her mouth hung wide open but powerless to do anything about it. Time seemed to stand still. She looked at Daniel as through a haze, saw his face alight with expectancy, and knew she ought to make some sort of response. "You—what?" she croaked.

"I know it's a bit sudden," Daniel began, "but when you think about it, it makes perfect sense."

Rachel stood motionless, waiting for him to explain how it could possibly make any sense at all.

"You've been knocking yourself out to keep things going and get the money you need to pay off the bank," he said. "You're working hard. Too hard. I have an idea that can help both of us. If you marry me, I can make the payment for you, and you can keep the farm."

Rachel's eyes narrowed. "You said it would help us both. What do you get out of it?"

Daniel stuck his hands in his pants pockets and swallowed. "Plenty. A home and a family and—"

"And my father's farm!" she shouted, hot tears spilling over to course down her cheeks. Decent and sincere she'd thought him. Had there never been an honorable man in the world save her father?

Daniel spread his hands, a look of bewilderment crossing his face. "Well, sure, I'd work the farm—"

"Leave me alone!" She bolted into the house, running past Violet to the sanctuary of her room and slamming the door behind her.

Lying across her bed, she let the tears flow unchecked. "Why?" she groaned aloud. "I thought he was different." All her earlier suspicions rose up to taunt her. Why hadn't she paid more attention to her initial misgivings? She had let Daniel sweet talk her, working hard and seeming trustworthy enough to make her think he only wanted to help. He had put on a good act, but it didn't make any difference now. No matter how upright Daniel had appeared, all the while he had only been out to get her land.

Rachel pushed herself to a sitting position, propping her elbows on her knees, and cradling her head in her hands. She should have known better. She could be honest in assessing her looks. . .or lack of them. Violet had turned out to be the beauty of the family. Rachel was the sturdy one.

She felt no shame in that; physical strength helped her get the work done. But she knew beyond a doubt she didn't possess the kind of allure that would make men flock after her. Certainly not enough to garner two proposals in as many days. Not for herself alone, at least.

To think she had felt chagrin at the way she had treated Daniel. Rachel writhed in mortification. What a fool she had been! What made her think she knew anything about men? Never mind. After Hiram's clumsy bid for her hand the day before and now this evidence of Daniel's perfidy, she now knew plenty about their scheming ways.

But he could have helped her save the farm. The thought teased at the corners of her mind and refused to go away. She rolled onto her side and curled her knees up under her chin. Had she made the worst blunder of her life in turning him down? In her heart, she knew marriage to be a sacred thing and not to be entered into lightly. But didn't love sometimes come later? Had she just bungled the one chance she and Violet might have to keep their home? Had her stubbornness and high ideals cost them everything?

"Rachel?" Violet's worried voice penetrated her awareness.

"Coming." She splashed water from her washbasin onto her face and blotted it dry. Violet didn't know about Hiram's proposal; maybe she wouldn't need to find out about Daniel's. If she hadn't acted like such a ninny, flying through the house that way, Violet wouldn't have had reason to suspect anything was wrong.

She opened the door, prepared to bluff it out. "Is lunch ready?" She tried to make her voice sound casual.

"Yes, but. . ." Violet paused. "I think something's wrong with Daniel. He saddled up and left without saying a word."

Rachel avoided her gaze. "He must have had some business to attend to."

"He didn't say anything about it earlier. And Rachel? He looked angry. Do you think he's coming back?"

"We'll just have to see, won't we?" Rachel sat down at the table and waited for Violet to join her before she asked the blessing.

Would Daniel return? Could she bring in the rest of the harvest alone if he didn't? Rachel pondered her dilemma while she ate. There wasn't much left to do, she assured herself. She could manage if she had to. She swallowed a spoonful of the soup Violet had made but tasted only the bitterness of Daniel's traitorous act.

Why should his leaving them to fend for themselves disappoint her so? She should feel glad his true motive had been revealed. What did it matter to her if he was no different than Hiram? The thought turned her stomach, and she left the rest of the soup uneaten.

eight

Rachel pulled her scarf close around her neck and pressed the tines of her digging fork into the garden soil. Giving the end of the handle a quick shove downward levered the tines back up, bringing a tangle of potatoes with them. She bent to knock off the dirt, then dropped them in her gunnysack and blew on her fingers to warm them.

The only thing certain about early fall weather in northern Arizona Territory, she thought wearily, was its unpredictability. Earlier that week she had enjoyed the warmth of the sun through her calico dress. Today, a biting wind stung her nose and fingers. She scanned the overcast sky, hoping the change in the wind didn't portend an early snowfall.

It had been two days since Daniel left. Two long, grueling days that made her doubt that she did have the stamina to make it through to the end of harvest. The warmth of the fireside tempted her, but this year above all years, she dared not leave one potato or carrot in the ground, one stalk of corn standing in the field. She shivered and bent to her task again, wondering which was harder to bear: the summer heat or autumn chill.

Violet had been pressed into resuming more of the simpler outdoor chores, leaving Rachel free to do the heavier work. After two days of silence, it seemed clear that Daniel had no intention of returning, and they simply couldn't fall behind. *Good riddance,* Rachel told herself, wishing her heart would join her head in celebrating his departure. He had shown his true colors at last, proving her instincts to be right all along. His absence shouldn't hurt so much.

She would get over it, she vowed, and be stronger for the experience. Next time she would trust her intuition and keep her distance from offers that sounded too good to be true. She couldn't risk losing her heart again, only to have it trampled underfoot another time.

With a sigh, she shouldered the digging fork and set off toward the barn, dragging the heavy sack behind her. Men like Hiram Bradshaw and Daniel Moore didn't merit the sorrow they caused. She used the back of her hand to dash away the tears that spilled from her eyes; she couldn't do a thing about the lump that clogged her throat.

Rachel dropped the sack inside the barn and gazed around the interior impatiently. Violet had been sent out earlier to tend to the milk cow, but the agitated lowing coming from the stall let Rachel know the animal hadn't been fed yet. And her sister was nowhere to be seen.

Probably off somewhere woolgathering, Rachel thought bitterly. Generally, she found Violet's dreamy nature entertaining, but seeing chores go neglected under the present circumstances made her fume.

"Psst." The soft hiss seemed to float out of the air over Rachel's head. She looked up to see Violet peering down from the hayloft.

"What are you doing up there?" Rachel demanded. If this was another of her sister's fanciful games. . .

"Shh. Not so loud. Come up here."

"Can't you come down?" Rachel softened her tone in spite of herself.

"Come on up, Rachel. Please."

She let out an irritated sigh. "Oh, very well." Why did she

let Violet talk her into these things? She heaved herself over
the edge of the loft and glared at her sister. "What now?"

Violet sat next to a mound of loose hay, watching a wrig-
gling mound of fur with a rapt expression. "Look at them,
Rachel. Aren't they precious?"

Rachel stepped closer and saw Molly stretched out on her
side, licking a tiny kitten with maternal pride. Her shoulders
sagged.

"There are eight of them," Violet whispered, oblivious to
Rachel's weary posture. She reached out to stroke the nearest
kit with one finger. "No wonder I couldn't find her; she'd
gone off looking for the best place to have them. Isn't it
exciting?" When Rachel didn't respond, she looked up. Her
face clouded over when she saw her older sister's lack of
enthusiasm.

"You're angry because I haven't fed yet, aren't you? I'm
sorry, Rachel. I'll get to it in just a few minutes, really I will.
I came up here to throw some hay down and found Molly,
and. . .I guess I just got caught up in the excitement of it all.
Please don't be mad."

Her plaintive tone cut straight to Rachel's heart. Daniel
had been right about one thing: Violet had experienced loss
too. No matter that Rachel now had eight more lives depend-
ing on her. How could she begrudge Violet this little bit of
joy when their world had been turned upside down?

With an effort, she forced a smile. "I'm not mad, Honey.
Just see to your chores before it gets too late, all right?"
Violet's look of gratitude dispelled some of her gloom but
didn't relieve her of her responsibilities. She descended the
ladder and picked up the corn knife, feeling like she carried
the weight of the world on her slim shoulders, and no one
seemed to care, except to add to it.

All through cutting and stacking the stalks of corn, Rachel wrestled with the ache of loneliness. Even if they could get over this hump and hire some help next year, would she be able to go on shouldering the full load of responsibility?

How she longed for someone to share the burden with. Someone who could help her bear it. Violet loved her dearly, but they didn't have anything like the same kind of partnership she'd had with Pa. Not like she'd hoped to share with a husband someday.

A heavy knot settled in the pit of her stomach. After what she'd been through in the past week, thoughts of matrimony ought to be the farthest thing from her mind. But her wayward thoughts had a will of their own, and images of Daniel flashed through her mind like scenes from a magic-lantern show. Daniel, with his strong arms hefting a load of firewood as easily as she could pick up Molly. The broad back muscles rippling under the taut fabric of his shirt. The concern in his eyes when she'd struck her head against the door frame.

What would it be like if he had proposed for the right reasons? She dismissed the thought as quickly as it came, berating her traitorous heart for daring to harbor such thoughts.

She propped the shock she'd just tied upright, secured the barn for the night, and made her way to the house, hoping she'd be able to stay awake long enough to eat and undress before she tumbled into bed.

nine

Daniel rode onto the Canfield property just after daybreak, his mouth set in a determined line. How many ways could a man manage to make a fool of himself? He seemed bent on trying to figure them all out. If it hadn't been bad enough to insult Rachel with his bright idea of marriage, skedaddling like a scolded pup only made him look like a bigger idiot.

In the three days since his hasty departure, he'd had plenty of time to sort things out. At first, he'd headed straight for his claim, aiming to use his newfound time to catch up on all the work he'd let slide while helping Ike's daughters. He'd aired out his roomy cabin and set about repairing a leak in the flume to his sluice box. Try as he might, though, he couldn't escape the memory of Rachel's face. She'd looked tired, so tired, and he hadn't even given her a chance to freshen up before he launched into his brilliant plan.

She'd wiped the dampness from her brow, and her hand had left a streak of dirt across her forehead that showed when she lifted her face to his. He remembered that and the way her clear brown eyes had clouded over when he made his inept attempt at solving her dilemma.

" 'I think we should get married.' " The arrogance of the blunt statement made him squirm with embarrassment. Had he really thought her so desperate she'd jump at any lifeline thrown her way? What a way to spring a life-changing idea on a woman! Even coming as a strictly businesslike proposal, he should have given her some warning of what

73

he intended to say.

These thoughts and more had eaten at him so over the past three days that the time he should have spent digging out a new pile of ore had been taken up with self-recrimination. As clearly as if she stood before him now, he could see the confusion written on her countenance, followed closely by disbelief, then anger. And he had put them there. As if she hadn't had enough to contend with, losing her pa, then working like a mule to make good on her loan payment.

She deserved a helping hand, and he had only added to her heartache.

Time alone with the Lord had given him a good opportunity to see his mistakes all too clearly. He'd learned something else during his absence. He missed Rachel. Missed her a lot, and that wasn't something he'd ever expected. Respect had turned into something far more tender, filtering into the background of his thoughts without him being aware of it.

His lack of experience in dealing with the fairer sex had never been more evident than when he spouted out his clever plan without ever thinking how it might sound to Rachel. If he had it to do all over again. . .but wishing wouldn't change a thing.

His biggest worry now—the one that drove away his appetite and kept him awake at night—was whether his colossal blunder had ruined any chance of ever regaining Rachel's trust. At this point, he hardly dared to hope for more.

Daniel unsaddled his horse and turned the gelding into the corral. Had he missed his one opportunity for happiness? He couldn't blame Rachel a bit if she never wanted to set eyes on him again. In her place, he'd probably want to pull that Henry rifle down from the wall and run him off the farm. On the other hand, the harvest still needed to be brought in.

A slow smile spread across his face. He liked having a strong bargaining point. She had to let him stay long enough to see it through. He wanted her to know that he followed through on his promises. Had she thought him a quitter the day he'd ridden off in a huff? The idea made him choke. It hadn't been like him to let his wounded feelings take over and goad him into deserting the sisters when they needed him.

Well, he was back to stay. . .at least until the harvest had ended. After that, only the good Lord knew, and Daniel had been bombarding heaven with pleas for divine direction.

His practiced eye scanned the fields, assessing what had been done in his absence. Rachel had been busy, he noted. She must have cleared another two acres. But then, had he expected anything less? She had shown him time and time again that she knew the meaning of hard work. The thought of her having to tackle it alone because he'd gone off to lick his wounds strengthened his resolve to stay. He would pitch in and finish the job, whether Rachel liked the idea or not.

"Daniel!" Violet ran down the porch steps and hurried to meet him. "Where have you been? We missed you."

"I had to check on some things back at my claim," he told her, flinching at the half truth. "But I'm back now and rarin' to go. I need to make up for lost time."

"Come to the barn with me," she said, tugging on his sleeve. "I want to show you what Molly's been up to."

"Found her, did you?" He smiled and followed her into the shadowy interior. Violet, at least, didn't mind his coming back. He began to relax a fraction.

&

Rachel heard Violet's glad cry and pulled back the kitchen curtain. She saw her sister fly down the porch steps and run across the yard in the early morning gloom. Even in the dim light, Rachel recognized Daniel's form at first glance.

Violet pulled at his arm, then led him into the barn. "Those kittens!" Rachel muttered. Her sister was besotted with them. Daniel didn't put up much protest, but why should she expect him to? Violet, with her captivating personality, could persuade almost anyone to whatever she wanted.

Rachel twitched the curtain back again in time to see the two of them emerge from the barn, laughing and talking animatedly. Daniel had lost the set look she'd seen on his face the last time they talked. Or rather, the last time she'd shouted at him. A pang of remorse smote her at the memory. Today he seemed to be at ease, more like himself. At least one of the Canfield sisters knew how to treat a person decently, she thought moodily.

She started to drop the curtain but caught sight of her reflection in the window glass and paused to stare at her image. A solemn face framed by light brown hair returned her gaze. Nutmeg-colored eyes looked back at her with sad awareness.

Rachel turned impatiently and went back to kneading biscuits. No wonder she only received proposals when they were motivated by greed. Why would anyone take a second look at her with a beauty like Violet around? Violet, with her vivid blue eyes and glossy hair the color of an otter's sleek coat, would capture any man's attention. . .and his heart.

Rachel knew she possessed pluck and determination, important traits for survival in this rugged land and things her pa had valued. But strength didn't attract suitors. Violet would always be the belle of the family; Rachel would fill her role as the one born to the land. She might just as well accept that.

❧

Daniel's mind churned while he started shocking corn. It

struck him as odd that he could know Rachel's strength of character so well and still have so little insight into the way her mind worked. If only there were some way to understand the way she thought.

Over by the barn, Violet set out a pan of milk for Molly. A smile touched Daniel's lips, remembering her excitement at showing off the cat and her new family. An idea started out like a wisp of smoke, then took shape in his mind.

Who knew Rachel better than her sister? He'd always found Violet easy to talk to; maybe he should cultivate their friendship more diligently. A few well-placed questions ought to put him on the road to making some headway with Rachel.

Understanding her was essential to the success of his newly formed plan. He fully intended to propose to Rachel again. And this time he wouldn't be offering her a marriage of convenience.

ten

The *clop clop* of the horses' hooves beat a steady rhythm on the hard-packed road, playing a counterpoint to the squeak of the wagon wheels. Rachel swayed in the wagon seat, her eyes drifting closed, then open again. The horses knew the way home and didn't need her constant attention, she reminded herself, gathering the reins in her fist.

She braced her feet against the foot board, then rested her forearms on her knees and allowed her eyelids to fall once more. She'd catch a few minutes' rest before she got back to the farm and resumed the endless cycle of cutting and tying the cornstalks into bundles.

Her shoulders sagged, and her head nodded in time with the wagon's rocking progress, but a tiny smile lifted the corners of her lips. Despite her weariness, the knowledge they'd made significant progress in recent days gave her reason to rejoice.

Just an hour ago, she had sold the last of the garden vegetables to Jake Samson. Earlier that week, Daniel had added fodder to the items they could sell to Fort Whipple. Tonight, if she could stay awake long enough, she'd enter the latest sales figures in her ledger and see how much farther she had to go to reach her goal.

Rachel dozed, rousing only when the horses slowed their pace at the turnoff to her property. She transferred the heavy reins to the other hand, flexing her stiff fingers and rubbing the sleep from her bleary eyes. As soon as she unhitched the horses and put the harness away, she could start clearing the old potato vines off the garden plot.

She rolled her head from side to side to stretch the complaining muscles in her neck. If Violet had remembered to prepare supper instead of getting sidetracked by some flight of fancy, she could look forward to a hot meal in an hour or so. If only she could hold out that long, there would be a brief respite from her labor.

But the next day would come, and the next day, and the next, each bringing with it an interminable list of jobs to be done. Rachel groaned aloud. Her former hopes for a break once the harvest was in had evaporated when she realized that in bending all her efforts to the task at hand, she had let any number of other chores go undone.

Firewood needed to be cut. The fields and garden needed to be plowed. Food set aside for their own use had to be put up for the winter. All these tasks still waited for someone to do them. Waited for her.

Would there ever again be a time when she could relax for more than a moment? A time to sit and plan and dream? The enormity of the job she had undertaken overwhelmed her. If she ever got caught up, perhaps she could sit and rest for awhile. Maybe until spring, when the ground thawed and the fields and garden were ready for planting. Maybe forever. Once she sat down in the rocker in front of the fire, she might never want to get up again.

At the barn, she pulled off the collars and traces and turned the horses out into the corral, envying their freedom at having the rest of the day to themselves. She hung up the heavy harness and headed for the kitchen garden.

On her way, she glanced toward the house, wondering what Violet had decided to cook. A stew would be nice, she decided. A stew rich with savory broth and fluffy biscuits on the side. She looked off toward the edge of the cornfield where Daniel worked to repair the deer fence and blinked. Her steps slowed while she tried to focus her tired eyes, unwilling to believe what she saw.

Two figures, not one, stood at the fence line. Daniel leaned against a post and appeared to be listening intently while the second person spoke and fluttered her hands in lively gestures. Rachel's eyes narrowed. She recognized the coat the other person wore. Violet. When she finished talking, Daniel threw back his head and laughed, then squeezed her shoulder. Violet gave him a playful swat on the arm in return and ran back to the house.

Rachel stood motionless so long she thought she might take root, then forced her unwilling feet to move and resumed her walk to the garden, her emotions in turmoil. Didn't she spend every waking hour working herself into the ground? How could these two take time to indulge in chitchat when the sun still shone and work cried out to be done? She just hoped Violet hadn't let their supper scorch. That would be the final straw.

This wasn't the first time she had seen them together. More than once she'd spotted Violet tagging along behind Daniel when she had business of her own to attend to. Her frustration mounted until she thought she would explode. Didn't either of them care about the looming deadline? Didn't they care about her?

She couldn't expect Daniel to worry about anything but his debt to her father. After all, that was the reason he had come to them in the first place. Even after his proposal. . .but she wouldn't think about that. Violet, though, ought to show some concern for what Rachel was enduring, especially since she did it not only for the two of them but for their father's memory.

A tight knot of despair formed in her chest, growing until it threatened to choke her. All the while she gathered up the withered vines, bitter thoughts ate at her spirit like an acid. By the time she walked back to the barn to put her tools away, she knew she had to resolve her angry feelings or burst.

Perhaps she misread the scene she had witnessed earlier. Maybe Violet had a legitimate reason for going to the field. She would go to the house prepared to give them both the benefit of the doubt. But if she discovered her earlier assumptions had been correct. . .

Lamplight streamed from the windows by the time she mounted the porch steps. Through the kitchen door came the sounds of lighthearted laughter. Rachel clenched her teeth, reminding herself not to jump to conclusions, and pushed open the door.

Daniel leaned against the far wall, watching Violet pull a custard pie from the oven. "If that tastes as good as it smells, it'll melt in your mouth." He smiled. "But you probably put in salt instead of sugar or threw the eggshells in the pie by mistake."

"Ooh!" Violet set the pie on the windowsill to cool and threw the dish towel she'd used to pull it from the oven at Daniel in mock outrage. "You just sit down and mind your manners. If you behave yourself during supper, I *might* let you have a piece." She turned to Rachel as if noticing her presence for the first time. "Have a seat. I'm ready to dish it up."

Rachel went to her room to wash, then settled into her chair at the end of the table. Violet set a steaming plate before her. The meal she had so anticipated slid down her throat unnoticed while she eyed her sister and Daniel.

"Not bad." Daniel patted his mouth with his napkin. "Even if I do hate to admit it."

Violet wrinkled her nose at him, then turned to Rachel. "Are you all right?" she asked, concern tingeing her voice. "You're awfully quiet."

"I'm fine," Rachel told her. "Just a little tired." *Like you two would be if you'd been working as hard as I have.*

Violet threw her a hurt look. "You didn't even say anything about the chicken and dumplings. It's your favorite."

Rachel glanced down at her plate. Was that what she'd eaten? She had been so busy watching the two of them, she hadn't even noticed. A twinge of guilt pricked her conscience. How could she stand in judgment of their behavior when her own had been so thoughtless?

"I'm sorry. It's delicious." She took another bite, just to be sure. It *did* taste good. What a pity she had been so absorbed with her resentful thoughts that she had missed this wonderful meal.

"I agree." Daniel eyed the plate on the windowsill hungrily. "Now, that pie may be a whole different story. . . ."

Violet narrowed her eyes at him. "If you're so sure it's going to taste awful, I'd hate to inflict any of it on you."

Daniel held up his hands. "Chivalry demands that I taste it first to protect you ladies from possible discomfort."

Violet sniffed but cut a slice of pie for each of them. Despite his teasing, Rachel noticed that Daniel received the biggest of the lot.

After pronouncing the pie an unexpected success, Daniel moved to the chair he had claimed as his own and leaned back contentedly.

"I'll be there in a minute," Violet called. "Just as soon as I clean the kitchen." She looked at Rachel. "Didn't you say you were going to tote up the ledger tonight?"

Rachel hesitated, torn between the desire to know exactly where they stood financially and her body's cry for rest. The need for sleep won out. "Not tonight," she told her sister. The total wouldn't change overnight, but she wouldn't be able to function tomorrow if she didn't get to bed.

Her exhaustion notwithstanding, sleep eluded her. Moonlight washed through her window, casting strange shadows on the wall. She stared at the ceiling, thinking over the events that had so upset her. Had she overreacted to a friendly conversation? In her fatigued condition, it was possible; she had to admit that. Maybe she'd been wrought up over nothing.

"Let all bitterness, and wrath, and anger, and clamour, and evil speaking, be put away from you, with all malice." She could hear the words of the verse as clearly as when Pa had read them by the fireside. Had the seeds of bitterness sprouted and taken root in her heart? *Lord, I'm sorry. It's just so hard. Please forgive me and help me not to fall prey to the snare of the enemy.*

Her eyelids fluttered closed, then snapped open again when a new thought struck her. What if the byplay she had seen indicated not a lack of concern for herself but a burgeoning interest in Violet? She sat bolt upright in bed, her heart pounding.

The idea unnerved her, and she swung her legs over the side of the bed, wide awake now. What had she seen that put that notion in her head? Pressing her fingers to her temples, she reviewed the events of the last few days.

Just how many times had she seen similar behavior and written it off to Daniel's patience with Violet's constant pestering? Going over the last week in her mind, she realized there had been other instances like that. Why hadn't she paid more attention to it before now?

Alarm welled up inside her, and she rose to pace the room. She shivered when her bare feet met the cold wood floor, but she paid it no mind. Her thoughts tumbled over one another in rapid succession. Could it be possible? Did Daniel feel an attraction to Violet?

Or was it the farm that held his interest? "If at first you don't succeed, is that what you're thinking, Daniel Moore?" If that were the case, she would make sure he never succeeded, no matter how hard he tried. She would have a long talk with Violet, tell her about Daniel's attempt to gain control of the farm through his earlier proposal. She would make her see she couldn't get involved with him.

Violet had never had a suitor. With her innocent, trusting nature, she would be easy prey for any unscrupulous cad who showered her with attention. But Rachel wouldn't let it happen. If that was what Daniel Moore had in mind, he could think again.

She climbed back into bed and pulled the covers over her, shivering in earnest now that her thoughts had slowed and she realized how cold she felt. Her mind whirled with imagined scenes in which she broke the news to Violet.

It wouldn't be easy. Violet had gotten used to having Daniel around. His presence helped to fill the void in her life left by her father's passing. Rachel closed her eyes, planning how she would phrase her speech. She would have to be understanding yet firm, gentle but uncompromising.

And somehow she would have to do it without alienating Daniel. She realized full well what a tricky situation she faced. Not only did she have to save the farm, she had to save her sister as well. And the man she had to save her sister from was the only one who could help her save the farm.

Rachel groaned, feeling as though she were about to try to pick her way along a path riddled with pitfalls.

Since Daniel's arrival, Violet had seemed happier than she'd been in ages. How could she impart such shattering news without crushing her fragile spirit? It would be hard to convince her of Daniel's perfidy when he appeared so relaxed and content in her presence, not stilted as he'd been with Rachel lately. A picture of their easy camaraderie earlier that night floated through her memory. Daniel's friendly banter showed he felt right at home.

A new, unsettling notion flashed into her mind. What if Daniel truly cared for Violet? Could this be the best possible way for things to work out. . .for Violet, at least? That proposition added a new dimension to her dilemma and robbed her of the possibility of getting any sleep that night.

eleven

Daniel let himself into the shack he now called home and struck a match to light the lantern. He shucked off his clothes and climbed into his cot. *It's been a good day, Lord. Thank You for all the work I got done and for everything I learned from Violet.*

He blew out the light and smiled into the darkness. Taking Violet into his confidence had been one of his better ideas. He'd feared her reaction at first, but her delight at helping him win Rachel matched his own at discovering her willingness to lend a hand.

She would make a good partner. Her enthusiasm for their joint effort heartened him, made him feel that finding a place in Rachel's heart wouldn't turn out to be the unattainable goal he had feared.

He couldn't tell just when it had happened and sure couldn't explain why. Letting down his guard and allowing a woman to get under his skin went against his grain, but he knew the truth in his heart: Somehow, God had determined that Rachel Canfield would be his. And if he had learned one thing, it was not to turn down a gift, no matter how unexpected, from the Almighty.

With a peaceful sigh, he rolled over and went to sleep.

ê

"You should have seen Molly carrying her babies down to the manger, one at a time. Maybe after two weeks with them up in the loft, she just wanted a change of scenery, do you think?" Violet lifted the tiny gray kitten from her lap and held him to her cheek. "Aren't they darling?"

Daniel unhooked the claws of its feisty black-and-white brother from his vest. The little animal batted his hand with its paw and hissed. "Darling. Right." He grinned and tapped a forefinger on the kitten's nose. It leaped down off his lap, offended, and tottered off to find its mother.

Daniel leaned back against the manger and watched Violet play with the litter until one by one they wobbled away in search of their supper.

The last kitten scampered off to join its littermates. "Look at the way Molly takes care of them," Violet said. "There's something special about the relationship between a mother and her young, isn't there?"

Daniel's peaceful mood ebbed away in a flash. He merely grunted a response.

Violet shot a questioning look at him. "What's wrong? You look like someone just hit you over the head."

His stomach bunched into a knot, and he willed it to relax. He'd never talked to anyone about this before and didn't know why he'd chosen Violet as his confidante, but the time seemed right. He stretched out one leg and hooked an arm around the other knee. "Maybe my ma should have been more like Molly," he began, long-suppressed memories teasing at the fringes of his mind.

"I don't ever remember getting a lot of comfort from her. Plenty of that, though," he said when Molly swiped a paw at one of the kittens, sending it head over heels. He forced a chuckle and avoided Violet's curious gaze. "Seemed like none of us older kids ever did anything that suited her." He toyed with a sliver of wood hanging from the manger. "She took off with a two-bit gambler when I was thirteen."

"How awful for you!" Violet's eyes grew round with compassion. "What kind of mother would go off and leave her children?"

Daniel shrugged. "Hard to figure. She took my younger brother with her but left me and my older sister there with Pa." He swallowed hard, trying to banish the remembered pain of the past.

"And you never saw her again?" Violet's tremulous voice called him back to the present.

He shook his head, remembering the hard times that followed. "Pa started drinking pretty heavy after that. Sis was four years older than me, and she jumped at the first chance to get married. She told me I could come live with her, but that didn't last long. I'd only been with them for a few months when she decided she didn't need an extra mouth to feed and booted me out."

Violet gaped at him. "How old were you then?"

"Nearly fifteen. I decided it was time to see what I could make of myself. It turned out I was good with horses and made a fair teamster. I found work with a freighter hauling goods to Santa Fe and just kept working my way west." He broke the sliver into two pieces, then four. "And that's how I wound up with a mining claim next to your father's." He tossed the fragments of wood in the air, trying to lighten both the mood and his load of memories.

"No wonder it's hard for you to trust women."

Daniel froze. Violet's quiet statement drove the breath out of him as effectively as a punch to the stomach. She regarded him with solemn eyes. He opened his mouth to contradict her, but the words wouldn't come. How could someone so young cut straight through to a truth he'd tried to hide, even from himself?

Violet leaned over and laid a gentle hand on his arm. "Rachel isn't like that, you know," she said, coming straight to the point once again.

One look at her told him there was no point in trying to sidestep the issue with this girl. He patted her hand. "I know." A relieved smile spread across his face, and he felt the wall he'd built around himself begin to crumble. "I know."

&

From across the yard, Rachel watched the exchange, trying to get a grip on her tumultuous feelings.

Who would have imagined Daniel playing with a bunch of kittens? Not her. She'd seen him only as a heaven-sent solution to their problem, then a land-hungry scoundrel, then the man who'd decided to pursue her sister. If she wanted to be truthful, she'd also seen him in a far more tender light, but she wasn't about to go into that now.

She crossed her arms and continued to observe them. Daniel spoke at some length, a succession of emotions playing over his face. Then Violet placed her hand on his arm and gazed into his eyes. Rachel almost choked when Daniel clasped Violet's hand in return. She pivoted on her heel and stormed off.

A very pretty scene, she thought, trying to throw off the guilt she felt at spying on something not intended for her eyes. *Very sweet and tender.*

Almost as tender as her own feelings. She stopped short, waving a hand in front of her face as though by doing so she could sweep away the sensations that raged within her. She had to stop this emotional tumult, the overpowering feelings of. . .

Jealousy? Toward *Violet?* The unexpected revelation staggered her, and she fought to catch her breath. It couldn't be. She felt concern about her sister's well-being. She only had

Violet's best interests at heart. Didn't she?

Shocked to the core at finding herself capable of such feelings toward her beloved sister, Rachel stumbled to the house and fled to her room. Chores could wait. The need to bring her bewildered state of mind before the Lord consumed her. Her relationship with Violet—and with the Lord—was more important even than the farm. She fell to her knees beside her bed.

Hands clasped and head bowed, she remained motionless for some time. The dreadful discovery had dredged up emotions so hateful, so ugly, she felt unable to voice them, even to her Savior.

"Father," she finally began in a faltering voice, "what is wrong with me? I thought I had done with thoughts of Daniel. I *shouldn't* think of him that way when I know he doesn't care for me." She drew a shuddering breath. "How can I—love Daniel," she uttered her admission with wonder and a tinge of shame, "when he's falling in love with Violet?" She covered her face with her hands, rendered speechless by her raw emotions.

"I love Violet, and I don't want to love Daniel. I don't want to—I *can't*—be jealous of their feelings for each other. Oh, Father, help me!"

She cried out to heaven with inarticulate sobs wrung from the depths of her innermost being. Throughout the tumult, a still, small voice whispered one word to her spirit: *Surrender.* With a mighty effort of will, she forced out the words, "Lord, I give my feelings about Daniel to You. Help me to want what's truly best for Violet. . .no matter what it costs me." The act of submission, of relinquishing her will to whatever her Father might ask of her, brought the awareness of victory, and with it, peace.

She pulled her tear-soaked hands from her face, wiping

them on the hem of her dress, then blotting her face with her apron. She kept to her room long after she would normally have been finished with her chores, knowing she didn't dare let Daniel or Violet see her swollen eyes and blotchy face.

The calm in her spirit assured her she had done the right thing. She just hoped she would be able to stay the course.

&

Daniel swung the axe high above his head, then brought it down with a loud *thunk* on the round of oak. He mopped his brow with his shirtsleeve. Nothing like splitting wood to work up a sweat, even at the end of October. Watching the mound of firewood grow filled him with satisfaction and pride.

He surveyed the pile of wood he'd already stacked in orderly rows. It would be enough to get the Canfield sisters through the next month or so, in his estimation. They'd need several cords more to see them through the winter. Daniel grinned. Plenty of reason for him to stick around awhile longer.

After that, he needed to hitch up the plow and turn the fields under before the ground froze solid. And after that, there would be plenty of other things a man could turn his hand to. He chuckled. Even with the crop finally harvested and delivered to market, there would be work enough to keep him there for months. He'd make sure of that, even if he had to create more jobs.

In his book, Violet deserved a prize for wisdom beyond her years. "Don't you dare leave once the crop is in," she'd admonished him, her eyes sparkling with excitement. "Spend as much time here as you can. If you're always around, she can't help but take notice of you."

Sound advice, he'd thought, and it seemed to be having an effect. He had noticed a definite softening in Rachel's attitude toward him over the past couple of weeks. If time would further his cause, he could stick it out however long it took.

He fetched the crosscut saw from its peg in the barn and set off to drop some more trees.

twelve

Rachel took special pains to compliment Violet on her supper of venison and potatoes. Once the dishes had been cleared away, she sat at the table and spread open her ledger. Before she wrote down the first number, she closed her eyes and sent up a quick prayer. It had been some time since she'd last totaled up the figures. Surely after all their hard work, she must be near the three hundred dollar goal.

She opened her eyes and set pen to paper, copying the notes she'd jotted on scraps of paper to remind her how much she'd brought in and for what. The column of figures grew.

Daniel sat in his favorite chair, feeding an occasional stick of wood to the fire. Violet, curled up on the hearth rug, snuggled three kittens on her lap. Rachel envied the cozy domestic scene and wished she could be more a part of it. Suppressing a sigh of longing, she rubbed her eyes with her thumb and forefinger and returned to her list of numbers.

Violet handed Daniel their father's Bible with a wistful smile. "Would you mind? Pa used to read from it in the evenings. I miss it."

Another thing she'd failed to keep up with. Rachel fought off the whispers of guilt and strained to hear Daniel's voice read from God's Word. For several moments, silence reigned, broken only by the sounds of her pen moving down the column in her ledger and Daniel flipping through the well-worn pages.

At last he cleared his throat. " 'Therefore I say unto you, Take no thought for your life, what ye shall eat; neither for the body, what ye shall put on. The life is more than meat, and the body is more than raiment.' "

He paused a moment, then went on. " 'Consider the ravens; for they neither sow nor reap, which neither have storehouse nor barn, and God feedeth them; how much more are ye better than the fowls?' "

Rachel's heart rejoiced at the comforting words. Being reminded that God really did care for her renewed confidence that He would come to their aid.

" 'Your Father knoweth that ye have need of these things.' "

She jotted down the last figure, then went back to the top of the column and began adding. Her brow knitted, and her stomach tightened into a knot. Two hundred and thirty-seven dollars. How could that be? She went back again, marking each subtotal on a separate piece of paper to be sure she hadn't made an error in addition.

She hadn't. She stared at the inadequate total. It still came out to two hundred and thirty-seven dollars. Rachel dropped her pen to the table and cradled her forehead in her hands. With the income from their hard-won harvest, the vegetables, and the eggs, they still fell far short of the amount they needed.

It didn't seem possible, yet the figures didn't lie. They had worked like troopers and done their best. And even so, the goal eluded them. Now they had no prospect of anything to sell save eggs and only six weeks to go until they reached the fateful time limit. Despite her best efforts, she had failed.

A soft moan escaped her lips. Would she and Violet really be turned out into the world alone and penniless, and in the middle of winter? She rose and made her way to join the others and sank into her rocking chair. Right now, she only felt numb. How long would that blessed numbness last before bitter reality set in?

She pressed her lips together to mask her distress. Both Daniel and Violet had their laps full of kittens. The little four-week-old balls of fur cavorted in wild abandon.

Violet laughed, enchanted by their antics, and Daniel smiled indulgently. "Try this," Violet said, reaching into the sewing box for two lengths of yarn. She handed one to Daniel and kept the other for herself. They dangled the strands above the kittens' heads, chortling when the little animals leaped at their targets.

Rachel rocked steadily, trying to distance her emotions from the happy group. She couldn't afford to become attached to Molly's babies. They might grow to depend on her, and she would only let them down too.

"Do you want to hold one?"

Rachel glanced down to see Violet offering her a gray-and-white kitten. "No." She saw Violet's look of disappointment and forced a smile. "I think I'll just sit and rock for a bit."

Violet nodded and resumed her game. Daniel set his little playmates on the floor, then stood and stretched. "Time for me to leave," he said. "We've all put in a good day's work. I'll see you in the morning."

Rachel only nodded and let Violet see him out and pull the latch string in for the night. She watched her sister stow the kittens with their mother in the dynamite box, formerly the home of the injured squirrel, and stoke the fire.

"Coming to bed?" Violet inquired, reaching to turn down the wick on the last lamp.

Rachel shook her head. "Go ahead. I'll be along after awhile." She listened to the sound of Violet's footsteps going to her room and heard the door close. Minutes later, the faint rustle of her mattress carried down the hall. Then the streak of light under her sister's door vanished, leaving Rachel alone with her thoughts.

The kittens ate their fill and settled down for the night after mewing and fidgeting a bit. She rocked and watched the fire burn down, a thousand thoughts tumbling through her mind. What could she have done differently? Could she have worked harder, accomplished more? She shook her head, despair seeping into every fiber of her being. She had done all she could, but she hadn't raised enough to meet the loan amount, let alone pay Daniel for all his labor.

One kitten, as wakeful as she, stood on his sleeping siblings and clawed his way to the top of the box. Hanging precariously from its edge, he teetered a moment, then dropped to the floor. The kitten crouched and looked about warily, then began exploring his surroundings.

"Better not," Rachel said and scooped up the little mite. She bent to return him to his bed, then paused and sat back in her chair, settling the tiny creature in her lap.

"Can't you sleep, either?" She traced the length of his body with her index finger and was rewarded by a soft purr. The kitten looked at her with unblinking eyes.

Rachel resumed her stroking. "What's keeping you awake, young fellow? You don't have a load of problems weighing you down." She ruffled his silky fur. "It's a good thing your food is taken care of by your mother, you know. You and your brothers and sisters may be the only ones around here who'll be eating before long."

The truth of her words struck home, and she swallowed hard. "It's hopeless." She forced the words past the unshed tears that clogged her throat. "Absolutely hopeless."

One tear, then another traced a slow trail down her cheeks. Folding her arms across her stomach, she leaned over and wept, the tears flowing freely. The kitten patted at her face with his velvet paw.

"I'd better put you back before you get soaked," Rachel sniffled. She returned the kitten to his bed, where he immediately curled into a ball and closed his eyes, the picture of contentment.

Rachel watched his even breathing, her shoulders slumped with fatigue. All well and good for the cats and Violet to slumber peacefully. They could rest without worrying about what tomorrow might bring, as in the passage Daniel had read. They didn't carry the responsibility of meeting anyone's needs like she did.

She had to go on, but how? And how could she rely on God to provide when He hadn't supplied the money they needed?

What had gone wrong? She remembered a time when she felt as carefree as the kittens, trusting in her pa to meet all her needs. Now she was the one who had to provide, and she knew her inadequacy for the task. She caught her breath in a ragged sob. It seemed she had all of life's heartaches and none of its joys.

🐾

Icy wind whipped through the pines and stung Daniel's face. He hunched his shoulders inside his sheepskin coat, glad for its protection against the elements. November in the mountains didn't show compassion to anyone.

He passed through the valley of Lynx Creek. Only a few more miles to go. Then he could get inside his cabin and build a fire to warm himself before he ventured outside again.

After all the weeks of endless labor, it went against the grain to take a couple of days off to check things on his mining claim, but he had to do it. If he didn't keep showing significant improvements, he couldn't prove up on it, and he'd ignored it far too long already. All the same, taking the time to do something strictly for himself struck him as self-indulgent.

The look on Rachel's face when he told her about his plans let him know she shared his thoughts. That surprised expression of hurt, quickly replaced by a mask of indifference, told him she wanted to protest, but her pride wouldn't let her.

Daniel knew he had no reason to feel guilty. He tallied up the work he'd done. Fifty acres of land had already been turned under, and split wood lay stacked in neat piles, enough to last them through the next three months. He'd worked hard, he reminded himself, and planned to work even harder.

He just needed to take this day to make sure of his claim. The gold he'd taken from the waters of the creek had provided him with a tidy income, most of which he'd managed to save by virtue of frugal living. If things went as he hoped, a steady yield would assume even greater importance. . .if he could persuade Rachel to marry him.

Had he made any progress toward that goal? At times he thought he detected a tenderness in her attitude toward him, but he couldn't be sure. Even ever-optimistic Violet didn't know what to make of her sister's frequent changes in mood.

He knew Rachel hadn't expected him to stay on once they'd completed the harvest, but she hadn't voiced any objection yet. He listed the jobs he'd outlined for himself. When he had cut enough wood for this winter, he'd start on next year's supply. Another thirty acres remained to be plowed and prepared for spring. Maybe he would have won Rachel's heart by then.

Failing that, he'd already made note of a number of things around the house and barn that needed maintenance and repair, things that Ike would have busied himself doing throughout the winter months. Rachel, though, might not have the time or the skills to take care of them. He had plenty of time to wear down her resistance, he assured himself smugly.

He topped a rise and looked down across the swale. Buckbrush and manzanita dotted the slope. In the spring, the whole meadow would be filled with lupine and Indian paintbrush. The scene never failed to fill him with a sense of wonder. The familiar feelings took hold now as he wended his way down through the trees. He glanced downstream. Abner and Seth Watson would be loading their sluice box, despite the bitter weather. He'd stop by their place first and see if they had any news to share.

Daniel pulled his gelding to a stop in front of the log-and-canvas shack, a crease forming between his eyebrows when he saw the sluice box sitting empty and no sign of activity. Normally, the two would have been hard at work since dawn. He scanned the area, a prickle of apprehension raising the hairs on the back of his neck.

It just didn't look right. Something had happened, he felt sure of it, but what? Unwilling to dismount and make himself vulnerable, he urged his horse forward and investigated more thoroughly. The only tracks he saw appeared to be days old and nothing gave any indication of foul play. Still, he couldn't shake the feeling that something had gone wrong.

"Abner?" he called softly. "Seth?"

Bushes rustled behind him, and he jerked his horse around, grabbing for his pistol.

"Daniel? That you?" Branches parted, and Abner Watson emerged from the brush, followed by his brother. Both looked as though they'd been holed up for days without sleep. "Man,

I'm sure glad to see you and not some painted Yavapai warrior."

Daniel stiffened. "What are you talking about?"

Abner bit off a chew of tobacco and rolled it in his cheek. "Apaches. We've been sitting tight for three days now, ever since Bill Stevens rode over to tell us they were running wild. Don't know whether they'll head this way or not, but a body can't be too careful."

Daniel's eyes widened. "I can't believe they'd risk taking on Colonel Kautz."

Abner nodded and spat into the bushes. "Surprised us too. We didn't expect any trouble, leastways not until spring. Kautz and his troops went off on some foray to the east, though, and this bunch of renegades decided to stir up trouble while they were gone. They've been going after some of the farms and ranches. Raided Zeke Johnson's place over near the Dells, Bill said."

Daniel thought sure his heart had dropped into his stomach. Its wild beating the next instant assured him it hadn't. He dug his spurs into the gelding's ribs and headed him back the way they had come.

"Ain't you going to check your claim before you go running off?" Abner's voice faded away behind him.

The claim would have to take care of itself. Getting back to Rachel was the important thing.

thirteen

Two hours later, he pulled his lathered horse to a stop in the Canfield yard. Rachel and Violet huddled over the washtub, scrubbing clothes vigorously.

Daniel turned his horse into the corral without bothering to unsaddle him and cupped his hands around his mouth. "Get to the house!" They looked at him, startled, and Rachel raised both hands in question. *"Now!"* he roared. His tone and actions would brook no argument, and they hurried to obey, dropping their laundry to the ground.

Daniel raced up the porch steps and slammed the door, dropping the heavy bar into place.

"What's this about?" Rachel bent double, panting after her headlong dash.

"Indians. What do you have in the way of guns besides the Henry? And where do you keep the ammunition?" He watched her lips form an *O* and saw Violet turn pale and press her hand to her chest. Given other circumstances, he would have broken the news more gently, but today he didn't have time to mince words.

Rachel didn't waste time asking questions but hurried to produce a shotgun and two pistols, along with boxes of shells. She lined them up on the table. "How long do we have, and what do you want us to do?"

Daniel felt a surge of pride at her matter-of-fact response. He couldn't spare a moment to tell her now, but when all of this was over. . .

"I'll take the front of the house. You keep watch out the kitchen window, and Violet can cover the back." He put action to his words, setting out weapons and piles of ammunition at each spot.

He turned to face the sisters, wanting to impress the seriousness of the situation on them without sending them into a panic. "Keep your eyes open for movement, shadows, anything at all out of the ordinary. Sing out the moment you notice anything unusual, whether you think it's important or not. I'd rather have a dozen false alarms than miss the real thing when it comes." He levered a shell into his rifle. "Thank God your pa cut down all the trees around the house when he built this place."

Rachel nodded solemnly. "I remember arguing with him when we first arrived, telling him I wanted at least some left near the house for shade." She flashed him a shaky smile. "I'm glad he didn't listen to me."

He sent them to their posts, repeating his instructions for good measure. They settled in, alert to the peril of their situation. Daniel filled them in on what he'd learned from Abner, as much to keep their minds occupied as to share information. Nerves stretched taut, they scrutinized every inch of ground within their view.

Hours dragged by and dusk settled like a fleecy blanket. From the bedroom Daniel heard a low rumble and Violet's embarrassed, "Rachel, I'm hungry."

"Why don't you put together something for us to eat," he called in a low voice. "Something light. We don't want the food to make us drowsy."

Rachel emerged from the kitchen long enough to hand each of them bread topped with a slab of venison. Daniel had just enough time to squeeze her hand and give her an encouraging wink before she hurried back to her post.

Daniel watched the shadows of the trees merge with the deeper darkness of night. "Might as well get some rest while you can," he told them. "I'll keep watch."

Rachel appeared in the kitchen doorway, hands on her hips. "We'll take turns," she stated, fixing him with a serious gaze.

He chuckled in spite of the tension. "Yes, Ma'am. But you go to sleep first. I'll wake you when it's time to take your shift."

The two women fumbled their way through the shadowy house and curled up side by side on a blanket near the cold hearth. Daniel made his rounds from window to window, thinking how much his life had changed in the past few months. He, who said he'd never wanted anything to do with another woman, now found himself responsible for two of them. And liking it.

ða

Long after Daniel called her to stand watch and lay down to get what rest he could, Rachel recalled the touch of his hand on hers when she handed him his spartan meal. Even while she moved from room to room, the memory of their brief contact gave her courage.

She blinked heavily. Her eyes felt as though grains of sand had rubbed them raw, and she had to fight to stay upright. The sky lightened by degrees, the inky blackness fading to an ashen gray, then to a pearly hue as the first pink fingers of dawn crept over the horizon.

She rolled her shoulders and shook her head to clear her mind. Nothing less than wide-awake vigilance would do now. While her gaze probed for movement among the trees and grasses, her thoughts strayed to Daniel again.

She felt his presence, warm and comforting, although she couldn't see him from her position by the window and didn't dare risk turning to get a glimpse of him.

He didn't have to be here. The thought echoed through her mind. She marveled, thinking about the ride he'd had. Knowing what time he'd left the day before, she calculated the distance he'd had to cover to reach his claim, then return. He must have pushed his horse to its limit to make it back so quickly. And why? He must really care for them—for Violet— to ride so hard only to risk his life to stand watch with them. That spoke of a courage and integrity that awed her.

He would make Violet a good husband, she thought, telling the pang of envy that swept through her to leave her alone. With Daniel around, she would never have to worry about her sister's welfare. That would be one less responsibility on her shoulders. If she did lose the farm, she would only have to concern herself with her own survival.

She blinked and nearly dozed, then caught herself. A distant drumming came to her ears and she stood erect, her pulse pounding in her ears. "Daniel?" she whispered.

"I hear it." He stood beside her in a second. They listened, straining to determine its source. Hoofbeats clattered into the yard.

"Hello, the house!"

Rachel flinched, then sagged with relief at the sound of the stentorian voice. Behind her, she heard Daniel lift the bar and open the door. Then came the scraping of boots on the porch. The next moment, Daniel stood beside her, gripping her shoulder excitedly. "They're gone," he told her, relief flooding his voice. "Tell Violet, then we can get something to eat."

Rachel rushed to do as she was bidden. Exhaustion threatened to overwhelm her, but the release from the night's tension buoyed her. She and Violet returned to find Daniel talking to two men.

"How do," the older one said, bobbing his head first to Rachel, then Violet. "Just wanted to let you all know the danger's passed. Someone got the word to Kautz's men, and they hotfooted it back here."

"So we're safe?" Rachel asked. With the release came weakness; her knees buckled, and she sank into a chair.

"Yes'm. They're going to continue regular patrols until they're sure things are under control and will stay that way." The man lifted a hand to the three of them, and he and his companion galloped out of the yard.

Violet moaned softly and swayed. Fearing she would collapse, Rachel helped her to bed, then returned to the front of the house.

Nearly dead on her feet, she stumbled into the kitchen where Daniel sat cradling a mug in his hands.

"I made coffee," he said, reaching over to pour her a cup. "Figured we both needed it."

Rachel dropped into a chair and nodded her thanks. She sipped the rich brew and gasped.

Daniel chuckled. "I figured I ought to make it plenty strong," he said.

"You succeeded." Rachel caught her breath and took another drink. No fear that she'd keel over now. This stuff would keep her awake the rest of the day. She looked at Daniel over the rim of her mug. "Is it really over?"

Daniel stared into the bottom of his mug and didn't answer for a moment. Finally, he nodded. "I think so. We'll stay close to the house today. We can go out to the barn when we need to, but only to do what's necessary for the animals. If we don't hear anything more by tonight, I think we can rest easy. As easy as a body can rest at a time like this," he added.

Rachel shook her head slowly. "I've taken a rifle with me every time I've gone into town alone for years," she said. "But Colonel Kautz and his troops have kept things so quiet, I never really expected to have a need for it. Up to last night, that is."

She rose to fix a hearty breakfast of scrambled eggs with bread and jam, not bothering to ration the eggs after their harrowing night. They ate in companionable silence, with Rachel thinking how natural it seemed to be sitting across the table from Daniel.

He lifted his gaze to her face, concern clouding his eyes. "Do you think Violet's all right?"

Rachel brought her wayward thoughts up short. Natural or not, she'd better not get any ideas about Daniel as anything but a future brother-in-law.

≈

In the week that followed, Daniel seldom left the property. After the threatened Indian raid, he'd spent a day putting up a crude shelter on the far side of the barn so he didn't have to be away, even at night.

Rachel felt grateful for his concern and slept better knowing he was never far away. She limited her visits to town to egg-selling trips only and kept the rifle close beside her all the way.

She found that Daniel's constant presence made for a mixed blessing. On one hand, it meant the opportunity to relax a bit, knowing she and Violet didn't have to defend their property alone. On the other, it made ignoring her feelings for him doubly difficult.

With winter coming on and fewer outdoor chores to do, Violet spent much of her time tagging along behind Daniel, talking to him nonstop. Rachel took over more of the cooking duties, resigned to her sister and Daniel forming a twosome.

She reached for the calendar hanging on the kitchen wall and marked off the day's date with an *X*. Another day. One day closer to the dreaded due date. Tears welled in her eyes.

Violet came through the front door, humming a lively tune. Rachel dashed the moisture from her eyes and busied herself cleaning the counter. She scrubbed the pine boards with an outward appearance of calm, but her thoughts continued to race. Twenty days remained until December 15 would be upon them. Less than three weeks, and she still fell nearly sixty dollars short of her goal.

Oh, Pa, if only I knew what to do! She looked around for something more to occupy herself. She had scoured every surface she could find, and still she needed some way to vent her pent-up anxiety.

"What are we going to do about tomorrow?" Violet queried.

Rachel blinked. "Tomorrow? What about it?" Her thoughts remained focused on a point three weeks away and the uncertain future that awaited them.

"It's Thanksgiving, you silly goose!" Violet fairly bubbled with excitement. "What are we going to do to celebrate? We've left off planning nearly too long as it is, but if we start now we can still do something nice. How many pies do we want, and what kind? I can start on the crusts—"

"We'll celebrate another time," Rachel interrupted before Violet got completely carried away. "Sometime when we have something to be thankful for." She watched the glow of anticipation fade from Violet's face and steeled herself for an angry outburst. When Violet walked away without so much as a word of protest, she heaved a sigh of relief.

Thank goodness she hadn't made a fuss. Rachel knew she

couldn't have dealt with any bickering just then. She leaned back against the counter and tried to figure out ways to bring in sixty dollars within the next twenty days. As far as she could see, it looked utterly impossible. Concern for their future weighed too heavily for her to feel festive or make any pretense of it. Not with the inexorable approach of the bank's cutoff date.

fourteen

Ten days later, the only thing that had changed was that the deadline loomed ten days nearer. Pellets of sleet peppered the windows, adding to the light skiff of snow that already layered the ground.

Rachel sat alone after supper, watching the fire and thinking over their situation. Violet had gone to bed early, giving her time to ponder her options. Ten more days remained until December 15. In just a week and a half, she would know whether the farm would belong to her or Hiram Bradshaw.

Her skin crawled at the very idea that man might ever look on her father's property as his. The memory of his face just after she'd pelted him with the rotten egg popped into her mind. A Christian young lady shouldn't enjoy the recollection so much, she supposed, but it might be the only satisfying remembrance she would carry with her in years to come.

She tallied the figures from the ledger in her mind. With the onset of winter, the hens quit laying as heavily. Mentally, she added up the number of eggs needed to make up the necessary difference, then shook her head. Even if they were laying at their peak, it still wouldn't be enough. A case of too little, too late.

A faint brush of sound on the wood floor caught her attention, and she turned. Violet stood in the doorway, looking like a little girl in her nightdress and robe.

"Are you sick?" Rachel asked, hearing the edgy tone in her

voice and hating it. She didn't think she could handle one more setback.

Violet shook her head. "I just wanted to ask you something." She crept farther into the room and stared at Rachel with soulful eyes.

Rachel braced herself. That look on Violet's face usually signified the prelude to a request for a favor. A big one.

"I know it's still nearly three weeks away," Violet said timidly, "but I wanted to know ahead of time. Are we going to celebrate Christmas this year, or are we going to skip it too?"

Rachel pressed her lips together and blinked her eyes against the sting of tears.

"I know we don't have money for gifts," Violet went on, "and that's not the point. It isn't the trappings, or the food, or even the time together." She moved closer and knelt by Rachel's chair. "It's the blessing of God's love, Rachel. The celebration of the gift of Jesus and everything He's done for us."

Rachel's throat constricted. When had her sister been so hesitant to talk to her before? And did she truly think Rachel would ignore the birth of their Savior? Come to think of it, though, why would she have any reason to believe otherwise, given Rachel's moody behavior of late?

She reached out and stroked Violet's head lovingly, painfully aware that it was the first tender gesture she'd made toward her sister in weeks. "Go to bed, Honey," she told her in a gentle voice. "And don't worry. We won't skip Christmas this year. . .or any other." The light in Violet's eyes warmed her as her sister brushed her cheek with a kiss and scurried back to bed.

The fire burned low, but Rachel continued to sit, deep in thought. Blessings, Violet had said. When was the last time she had looked for blessings?

When had there last been any? a rebellious part of her mind queried. It didn't seem like God had done much of anything *for* them lately, although He'd allowed plenty to happen *to* them.

When did I become so bitter? Maybe that was a better question, the answer to which might prove revealing. Rachel covered her face with her hands. *What would Pa have done in these circumstances?*

I remember what it was like when he was alive, she mused. *I remember what it was like to feel happy.* Pa had always taken time to sit with her and Violet in the evening, reading to them from the Bible and talking to them about what had happened that day. A wistful smile curved Rachel's lips, remembering how he had listened patiently to their girlish questions and dreams.

How had he managed? Had times always been easy for him? She pondered the question with new insight. No, they hadn't. She could remember plenty of struggles without even trying.

What, then, made his response to life so different from her own? Her glance fell on the Bible on Violet's chair, and she reached for it with a tentative hand. Without question, she knew where Pa had found his strength. Hadn't he told her time and again that she could trust God no matter what?

She thumbed through the well-worn pages, trying to remember some of Pa's favorite passages. The pages opened of their own accord at the book of James. Rachel scooted her chair closer to the lamp and studied the words. "My brethren, count it all joy when ye fall into divers temptations. . . ."

She stared in disbelief. Joy? How could she count it joy when she felt so tired she could barely move, when she'd worked harder than she ever believed she could and yet saw nothing but destitution staring them in the face? What joy awaited them in knowing that unless a miracle occurred, Hiram Bradshaw would soon be the owner of Pa's farm? And was she supposed to find happiness in his vulgar treatment of her? Rachel cringed at the recollection of his leering face. Happiness? She thought not.

"Knowing this, that the trying of your faith worketh patience." Pa had penned a note in the margin, and she strained her eyes to see it in the lamplight. She turned the pages eagerly to 1 Thessalonians 5:18.

"In everything give thanks; for this is the will of God in Christ Jesus concerning you."

Rachel stared into the flames, seeing, not the dancing colors, but Pa's face. Pa, who must have been incredibly tired himself, yet found time to listen patiently to the chatter of two growing daughters. Pa, smiling even when he faced adversities as big as her own. Comprehension filtered into her awareness slowly. Pa hadn't found joy *because* of his circumstances but *in* every circumstance.

He didn't have it handed to him on a silver plate. He chose to take God at His word and be happy. *He* chose *that. . .and I can too.*

She closed the Bible and hugged it to her, turning this new idea over in her mind. She could choose to trust God no matter what—whether she and Violet lost the farm, whether Violet married the man who had won Rachel's heart. She could do all things through Christ, who gave her strength. With His help, she would weather any storm life sent her way.

She tightened her hold on the Bible and turned her eyes toward heaven. "Thank You, Lord," she whispered. "I choose joy."

⅜

The next morning dawned fine and clear. Rachel dressed warmly for her trip to town, knowing the drive would be cold, but grateful that yesterday's snow had already vanished. She packed the eggs carefully, layering them between towels in the basket, then wedging the basket between a pair of blankets to guard it against any bumps along the way.

"Do you want to come along?" she asked Violet, who had come out onto the porch to see her off. Violet blinked at her buoyant tone but declined. Rachel gave her a cheery wave and drove off, leaving Violet staring after her in amazement.

Moments after she reached the road, she pulled the rifle into the seat beside her instead of its customary spot in the back. The vigilant efforts of the troops at Fort Whipple seemed to be having an effect, but it wouldn't pay to be careless.

The crisp air nipped at her cheeks and nose. Rachel tipped her head back and inhaled its sweet freshness, wondering at her ability to enjoy the day when she knew this might be the last trip she made to town as the owner of the farm. It seemed the whole world had changed since last night, but she knew the biggest change had taken place within her.

Nearly an hour from home, a tiny cry caused Rachel to sit up straight, her mouth suddenly dry. Indians often imitated animal sounds. Had that been a signal? She tightened her grip on the reins, not sure whether to pull the horses to a stop or urge them into a run. She heard the sound again and turned to the wagon bed behind her, feeling a mixture of relief and irritation.

One of the kittens reached out from its nest in the blankets and swatted a paw at her hand. Rachel sighed in exasperation. "How did you get in here? You must have jumped in just before I left." She scooped up the tiny creature and held it on her lap, considering. She'd gone too far to turn back now and return the baby to its mother. Little as she liked the idea, the kitten would have to travel to town with her.

She reached back to settle the stowaway again, pulling the blanket folds around it to form a warm nest. "Better stay put," she warned. "It's cold out here." She clucked to the horses and set off again.

Pulling the horses to a stop behind Samson's General Store, she jumped to the ground and brushed the wrinkles from her skirt. She would go in with her head held high. No one else needed to know how important every sale would be over the next few days.

Jake Samson looked up from the counter and beamed. "Pleasure to see you, Rachel. I was wonderin' whether you'd stop by soon. I've been out of your eggs for days, and I've had customer after customer pestering me about them."

Rachel fixed a smile on her face and set the basket on the counter. No need to tell Jake his egg supply might soon disappear.

"Fact is, the demand's been so high, I decided to raise my price." He gave her a conspiratorial wink. "I'm going to pass some of that along to you."

Her heart leaped, and she had to force herself to wait until she reached the privacy of Jake's back doorway to count the money he handed her. It wouldn't do to appear too eager.

She dropped the last coin into her hand and felt disappointment creep into her heart. The amount came to more than she'd hoped for, but it still didn't give her enough. *Trust in the Lord,* she reminded herself, trying to recapture her earlier gladness.

Rachel squared her shoulders and marched out the door to the wagon. She stopped abruptly at the sight of a grizzled miner standing next to the wagon box.

He started when he saw her, and a red flush suffused his face. "Beggin' your pardon, Ma'am." He ducked his head and scuffed his boots in the dust. "I didn't mean no harm. I was just lookin' at your kitten here." He held up the gray ball of fluff that Rachel had forgotten until that moment. "Cute little feller, isn't he?"

"I–I suppose he is." The kitten's charm had been lost on Rachel in the light of her present worries. Apparently the miner didn't share her lack of appreciation.

"Smart one too," the miner went on. "Watch this." He trailed his finger along the wagon bed and laughed out loud when the kitten pounced, swatting his hand fiercely. "See? He's a real feisty one."

A smile tugged at Rachel's lips. She had to admit he had a point. Nice to know that something could lighten her load of troubles, if only for a moment. She sent up a quick prayer of gratitude.

"Yes. Well, I need to be going now." She put one foot on the wheel hub and stepped up into the seat, hoping the man would take the hint.

He leaned over and placed the kitten in the wagon box with tender care but continued to stand with his hands on the side of the wagon. Rachel chafed, needing to be on her way but not wanting to appear rude.

The miner looked up at her with rheumy eyes and cleared his throat. "Beggin' your pardon, but I'm wondering if there's any way you could part with that little rascal."

He held up a hand to forestall any protest and continued. "I know you're probably real attached to him, and I'm asking a lot, but Ma'am, it gets mighty lonely out on the claim with only myself and my mule to talk to. If I could have this little feller with me, it would help a lot." He peered into Rachel's face like a child begging for candy.

She suppressed a laugh. Having one kitten less would lighten only a fraction of the load she bore, but even that would be an encouragement. She smiled. "Take him. I'd like for you to have him."

The man's face lit up in a snaggletoothed grin. He lifted the kitten from its nest of blankets and held it close to his chest. "You and I are gonna be pards," he crooned. "You like that idea?" The kitten responded by snuggling against his checkered shirt and purring loudly.

"You see that?" he asked triumphantly. "The little feller likes me already. Thank you, Ma'am. You've made me a happy man today."

Rachel smiled and nodded. She lifted the reins, preparing to leave, but the miner held up his hand again. "Wait a minute, Ma'am. I need to give you somethin' for him." He fumbled inside his coat, then pressed a lumpy object into her hand. "May the Lord bless you for your kindness." He dipped his head in farewell and walked away, cuddling the kitten against his scraggly beard.

Amused by the picture, Rachel opened her hand. A small leather bag rested in her palm. She tugged at the string tying the top together. The pouch fell open to reveal a small pile of glittering dust.

Rachel gasped. Gold? She glanced around to make sure no one else had seen, then tucked the poke inside her coat pocket before clicking her tongue and turning the horses toward home.

Once she'd gotten out of sight of Prescott, she pulled out the bag again and hefted it in her hand. Remembering similar pokes Pa had shown her, she estimated it to weigh about an ounce.

Quickly, she calculated its value. It put her nearly twenty dollars closer to her goal. It wouldn't make up the whole difference, but it would provide a little help for her and Violet while they looked for a place to stay and some means of support.

The income brought in from the harvest would go to the bank—she didn't intend to leave any more of Pa's debt unpaid than she could help. But this could be considered "found" money, something supplied by God to take care of their needs.

"Thank You, Lord," she whispered. Laughter welled up in her throat and burst from her lips in a joyful gurgle. "Thank You for Your provision and for letting me know I can trust You."

fifteen

The next day found Rachel pitching hay down out of the loft, humming one of her favorite hymns. Violet appeared in the barn doorway. "There's someone here to see you," she said with a curious look. "He says Tom Dolan sent him."

"Dolan?" Rachel tried to recall anyone by that name but couldn't. Mystified, she followed Violet out to the yard, where the man awaited her. His tattered clothing and heavily laden mule gave away his occupation before he could speak.

"Morning, Ma'am," he said, removing his hat. "Tom Dolan told me to come see you, and Jake Samson told me how to find your place. Tom got a kitten from you yesterday, and I wondered if you might have more to sell." He wet his lips and stared at her, looking as eager as a schoolboy.

Rachel recovered from her surprise and shot a warning look at Violet. "They're in here," she told him calmly, leading the way into the barn.

The threadbare miner took his time inspecting the litter and finally selected the biggest kitten. "Looks like she'll make a good mouser." He grinned. "I surely do thank you," he told her and produced a bag identical to the one Tom Dolan had given her the day before. "Here. Tom said this was the going rate." He grabbed the mule's lead rope and started to walk off, then stopped. "Do you mind if I spread the word about them others?" he asked. "I know a bunch of fellers who'd be glad of a little company like that."

Rachel started, then rallied. "Go right ahead," she called,

ignoring Violet's dumbstruck expression. "We'll be glad to see them." She gave her sister an exuberant hug. "God's in control, Violet. Isn't it wonderful?"

❧

By the following afternoon, Rachel and Violet were once again the owners of only one cat, Molly. Rachel sat at the table, lining up their money in neat piles, then checking the total against the amount in her ledger. She blinked incredulously. Three hundred and eighty-one dollars. Far more than she needed to pay off her debts. Enough to give Daniel a share for all his hard work. Enough to see her and Violet through the next few months.

And enough to make this a special Christmas for her sister. Joyful tears sprang to her eyes and spilled down her cheeks. "Thank You, Lord, for what You've done," she prayed. "Forgive me for doubting You, and help me always to know that You're in charge of my life."

She might have missed the official holiday, but songs of thanksgiving rang in her heart. Reaching for her pencil, Rachel sorted the amounts from the various sources and added them up. She tapped the end of the pencil against her teeth and studied the paper. Everything they had done had played a part in their success—the corn, the kitchen vegetables, the unexpectedly lucrative eggs. They would be sure to continue all of them next year. But those kittens. . .

Rachel sprang to her feet, shoved her arms into her coat sleeves, and hurried out to the barn. Violet poked her head outside just as Rachel tucked the old sewing basket into the wagon. "What are you doing?" she called.

"I have an errand to run," Rachel replied and got the team moving. She had to do this before she changed her mind. If she took time to explain her mission to Violet, she might talk herself out of it.

She drove the team at a brisk trot along the frost-covered road, not slowing until they came to a shabby-looking place. Rachel stopped the horses in front of the run-down cabin. Hooking her arm through the basket handle, she marched to the door and rapped on it sharply. A moment later, a seamed face appeared in the doorway.

"Miss Rachel?" Jeb McCurdy's eyes widened ludicrously at the sight of his neighbor. He hurriedly smoothed his hair back with both hands and hitched his trousers a notch higher. "What can I do for you?"

Rachel lifted her chin and moistened her lips. "I've come to make you an offer on your tomcat, Mr. McCurdy."

"On my—" The old man's mouth dropped open. "Miss Rachel, are you joking?"

Rachel tapped her foot in irritation. "Of course not. I'm perfectly serious. I'm talking business here. Are you interested or not?"

Jeb McCurdy rubbed a gnarled hand over his grizzled beard and regarded her thoughtfully. "Seems to me, the last time you saw my cat, you called him some powerful unfriendly names. 'Wayward' and 'wanton' came into it, if I recall." His eyes narrowed. "And now you want to pay good money for him and take him home with you, is that it?"

Rachel felt a blush heat her face but held her ground. "That is correct. I wish to purchase your cat."

Minutes passed while her neighbor eyed her thoughtfully. "The thing is, I just have to wonder what on earth you want with him, you taking such a dislike to him earlier and all." A glint of suspicion sparked in his eyes. "Cats make good tamales, I hear. You ain't planning to eat him, are you?"

"Of course not." Rachel gagged at the revolting idea. "I simply feel that he might be of some value to me. . . ."

She let her voice trail off, unable to find the words to explain her plan.

A moment of silence ensued, followed by a wheezing laugh. Jeb McCurdy's shoulders shook with glee. "So you decided there's something the old boy's good for, after all, eh?" His face contorted with suppressed mirth, then he leaned against the doorjamb and howled. "If that don't beat all!"

Rachel drew herself erect. "Are you willing to sell him or not?" she asked, her voice laced with impatience.

Jeb McCurdy caught his breath and wiped his watering eyes. "Oh, I'll sell him, all right. He doesn't stay around here half the time anyway, and now I won't have to worry about you coming after me every time he shows up on your place. What are you offering?"

Rachel held out a handful of silver, and the old man reached for it with a smile. "Just a minute," Rachel said, drawing her hand back. "The price includes the cat, caught and confined in this basket."

McCurdy looked as if he wanted to argue, then shrugged and pulled on his coat. "Come on, little lady. Let's go find your tom." He pocketed the money, then looked straight at her. "I want the pick of the first litter," he said with a knowing wink.

Thirty minutes later, she drove back into the yard, basking in her sense of accomplishment. Violet hurried out to greet her, pulling her shawl tight over her head and shoulders. "Where have you been?" she demanded. "And what's that noise?" She pointed to the wicker container, from whence an outraged yowling emanated. Her brow puckered in consternation. "Rachel, you haven't been doing anything to Molly, have you?"

"Help me fix up a place in the barn, and I'll explain."

Rachel led the way into the barn, where she proceeded to fashion a sort of cage out of several old crates. When she felt satisfied, she held the mouth of the basket to the opening and released the catch on the lid. Out sprang the wide-eyed tom, his fur standing on end.

Violet gasped. "Rachel, what on earth—"

"He's a business investment," Rachel told her smugly.

Violet goggled at her. "Investment? You don't mean you spent good money on that creature, when you've been so worried about making ends meet?" She put her hand on Rachel's forehead.

Rachel laughed happily and brushed her hand away. "I'm learning, Violet, that God's provision comes in various forms, some of them quite unexpected."

❧

The streets of Prescott bustled with activity. Rachel took her time stepping down from the wagon and meticulously straightened the lines of her best wool dress. Taking a firm grip on her reticule, she walked through the bank's doors and headed straight for Ben Murphy's office.

"Good morning, Ben," she called through the open door. "I need a moment of your time."

"Rachel, it's good to see you." The banker rose from his desk and hurried to greet her. His smile of greeting warmed her, but she could also see the worry in his eyes and realized he didn't expect her to make the payment. *He thinks I've come to beg for more time and doesn't know how he'll tell me no.* She smiled in return, planning to enjoy her moment to its fullest.

Ben pulled a leather-covered chair closer to his desk and seated her in it with a solicitous air. "How have you been, Rachel?"

"Pretty well," she replied. "We've been working hard, you know."

"Ah, yes." Ben's smile lost a fraction of its brightness, and he folded his hands together, tapping his thumbs nervously. "There's a lot to running a farm. Especially when you're trying to do it single-handed."

"That's true," Rachel agreed, maintaining her solemn expression. "Ben, it's almost Christmas. . . ." She allowed her voice to trail off.

He swallowed hard, his Adam's apple bobbing up and down behind his starched collar. "I know, Rachel, and don't think for a minute I don't sympathize with your plight. It's just that—"

"So I hope this will make your holiday a bit brighter." Rachel reached into her reticule and produced a thick envelope. She laid it in the center of Ben's desk with a flourish.

Ben's mouth dropped open, and he gawked at it in a most undignified manner. "What–what's this?"

Rachel stifled her inclination to laugh. "It's the money we owe you," she said in her most formal tone. "All of it. The amount of both notes, paid in full, and nearly a week ahead of schedule."

Ben closed his mouth and swallowed. He opened it again and tried to speak, but no words came out. He pulled a snowy handkerchief from his coat pocket and dabbed at his forehead. Finally he managed, "But how. . . ?"

"God's grace," Rachel replied softly. "It's His provision, pure and simple."

Ben nodded, still staring unbelievingly. After counting the money, he wrote out a receipt and handed her the cancelled note. "Congratulations. It's all yours now, free and clear."

Rachel left the bank, blinking back tears of joy. She stood

on the boardwalk and surveyed the scene before her with heightened appreciation. The broad expanse of the plaza, the false-fronted buildings, and the wide, dusty streets held a beauty she'd never noticed before. Even the gunmetal gray of the brooding winter sky couldn't dampen her euphoric mood.

She had done it. No, *God* had done it. She could hardly believe her ordeal had finally ended. The new sense of freedom seemed too good to be true. With a light step, she walked to the wagon and stepped up on the wheel hub.

"Trying to beg a little more time off Ben, are you?" Hiram Bradshaw's raspy voice came from directly behind her.

Rachel spun around and slipped off the wheel hub. She caught the side of the wagon to keep herself from toppling over and winced when splinters from its rough edge grazed her fingers. Pressing her hand against her dress, she ignored the hurt and glared straight at Hiram. Not for anything would she let him know she felt pain.

"As a matter of fact, you're wrong again. I've just paid off my loans. Both of them. The farm belongs to me, Hiram, and there's nothing you can do about it."

Hiram snorted. "Nice try, but I happen to know there's no way you could have come up with the money." He sneered and leaned against the wagon as though they were having a civil chat.

"There are ways higher than ours," Rachel told him, her joy overshadowing her distaste for his company. "Maybe this will convince you." She held the cancelled notes out for him to see.

With a look of disbelief, Hiram wheeled toward the bank. She could hear him bellowing Ben's name even after he entered the building.

sixteen

Rachel drove home in a blissful haze. Now that the load of responsibility had been lifted from her shoulders, she felt as though she might float right up to the top of Granite Mountain. Even her fingers had ceased to pain her. She threw back her head and laughed, causing the horses to prick their ears in her direction. "There's nothing to worry about," she called to them. "I'm just making a joyful noise."

While the team carried her home, she made plans for the coming year. With the extra money provided by the sale of Molly's kittens, she could buy additional seed and plant another twenty acres. That would cover the expense of hiring workers to help bring in next fall's harvest and still leave her and Violet with a tidy profit.

On top of that, she now knew her eggs could bring in enough to take care of most of their household expenses. And she had her newly acquired ace in the hole, Jeb McCurdy's tomcat. Any litters he and Molly produced would mean extra income they could put by for emergencies.

It meant freedom, she thought, reveling in the heady feeling of independence. No longer would she have to depend on Daniel and his sense of duty to her father. His debt had long since been discharged. He could pursue his mining interests, unhindered by any onus of responsibility toward them.

The thought of him leaving filled her with sorrow, but she knew God could take care of that part of her life too. She focused on her trust in Him and resolved to ignore the only dark cloud on her otherwise happy horizon.

&

Violet celebrated their release from debt by making a special supper of fried chicken, beans, mashed potatoes, and gravy. Conversation lagged at the table while the three of them savored the delicious meal.

Afterward, Rachel sat in her customary place by the fireside, wanting to enjoy an evening free from the hectic pace of the past months.

She glanced toward the table, where Daniel and Violet still sat engaged in an animated conversation. Rachel watched the glint of the firelight on their heads, one fair, one sable, and thought what a handsome pair they made.

She had to admit Daniel had been very good for Violet. Her sister had regained her vivacious spirit and had a sparkle in her eyes Rachel hadn't seen since before Pa's death. Rachel noticed a new lilt in her voice and spring in her step, as well.

Daniel too seemed different. Instead of the wary man Rachel saw when he first arrived, his eyes now held a flash of hope and determination. He looked like a man with a purpose, and Rachel knew full well what that purpose was.

How long would it be before he asked her permission to marry Violet? A sense of dread gnawed at her stomach, one she couldn't disregard.

Looking at it from a practical standpoint, it made perfect sense. The two of them could settle in Prescott, where Daniel could keep Violet in fine style as well as work his mining claim. It would give Violet the kind of home life Pa had wanted for her. And it would free Rachel from having to worry about more than just the farm and herself.

She could spend her days on the place she loved. . .alone. Rachel picked up some mending and concentrated on threading her needle, determined not to give in to the loneliness that beset her without warning.

After all her hard work to keep the farm, the prospect of having it all to herself seemed unaccountably bleak. What would her life be like without Violet around? It wouldn't be like she'd lost her sister, she admonished herself. Violet would still live nearby, close enough that they could visit frequently.

Rachel shot another glance at her sister, who listened to Daniel with rapt attention, then nodded eagerly. She seemed smitten enough with him, but then, who wouldn't? Rachel allowed her gaze to roam over his strong features, taking in the sandy hair bleached even lighter by the sun, the forest-green eyes, and the small cleft that softened the determined set of his chin.

How could any woman in her right mind not be attracted to him? If his physical appearance alone wasn't enough to capture attention, what about the character he had shown when he set himself to work unpaid for two young women he didn't even know?

Daniel patted Violet's hand, and Rachel smiled wistfully. He had only come to pay a debt. And she had only intended to let him. She'd never expected him to become such a per-manent—and treasured—fixture in their lives.

Her mind flitted back to the day Daniel made his proposal. Looking back, she now believed he'd meant exactly what he said—he had only wanted to help them both. Her eyes grew misty. What would have happened if she had accepted his proposal and agreed to marry him? A shiver of delight ran up her spine.

No! She caught herself up sternly. She would not, would *not* dwell on idle dreams of what might have been. Not when his offer had been based on pity and not on a true desire to have her as his wife. Not when he was now the man Violet loved.

She stabbed the needle through the fabric with angry, jerky movements. These foolish fancies wouldn't do. She had determined before God to follow the right path and wish for her sister's good. She could only assume He had shown His will in providing a husband for Violet in this unexpected way.

At sixteen, Violet was undeniably young, but not so young she couldn't marry. Rachel had known plenty of girls who'd said their vows at that age. The surprise she felt that Violet would be getting married first rankled her. She'd always assumed it would be the other way around, with her being older and all, but who said it always had to happen that way?

She would endorse Violet's choice with a smile, giving her all the support she could muster. And somehow, she would get used to thinking of Daniel as her sister's husband.

&

The knife blade passed along the whetstone a final time. Daniel tested it with his thumb and smiled. Good and sharp. He had always had a knack for honing a tool to its keenest edge.

Careful of the razor-sharp blade, he carried the knife toward the house. Rachel had complained about its dullness only the night before. She should be pleasantly surprised by his good deed.

He had taken Violet's advice to heart and stayed around the place, making himself useful and keeping Rachel aware of his presence. Piling up firewood and mending tools and harness hadn't gone unnoticed by her, but he wanted to do something that would affect her more personally. A sharpened knife was a small thing, but it would be a start.

While the harvest was underway and they'd scrabbled to pull together every cent they could, he had held off on making major overtures to her. She'd had all she could handle then just trying to keep things going, and he saw no point in overburdening her. But now that she'd been freed from the pressure of the loan, Daniel felt the time had come to move forward.

He entered the kitchen and found Rachel, hands on her hips, staring at a loaf of freshly baked bread.

"Have you seen—" Her eyes widened when he held out the knife.

"Looking for this?" He grinned at her surprise. "Watch out for that blade," he cautioned when she reached for the handle. "It's sharp."

She tapped the edge with a cautious finger, and her face creased in a smile of delight. "Just what I needed!" She gave him a grateful look and began to slice the bread with easy strokes. "Just for that, how would you like some bread and jam?"

"Throw in a glass of milk, and you've got a deal." He watched her set a crock of butter on the table beside the bread, then reach for the jam jar. Even doing simple kitchen chores, her movements were smooth and graceful. *Easy on a man's eyes,* he thought. Something he could enjoy watching for a long time—like the rest of his life.

He tried to hide his pleasure when she poured two glasses of milk and sat down across from him. No point in scaring her away, not when he'd just started making progress. He searched for something to say.

"How does it feel to be half owner of the finest farm around?" The question seemed safe enough, given their recent celebration.

Rachel took a moment to spread jam evenly over her

bread, then smiled. "Actually," she said, propping her elbows against the edge of the table and lacing her fingers together, "I'm the full owner. Pa left it all to me." Her smile broadened. "Violet isn't tied to the farm in any way." She popped a bite of bread in her mouth and chewed, a pleased expression spreading across her face.

Daniel pursed his lips and let out a low whistle. Why didn't it surprise him that Ike would leave his property in Rachel's capable hands? Her father had been well aware of her love for the land.

Rachel finished her bread and took a drink of milk. Daniel couldn't help but chuckle. She'd tilted the glass a little too high, and a thin white line decorated her upper lip.

He picked up a napkin and swiped at her lip. "Just wiping off your mustache," he said in answer to her startled look. He reached out to blot her mouth again. It felt good to be so close to her, to feel her breath brush across his hand. And she didn't need to know he'd gotten every bit of milk off her face the first time.

He polished off his milk with one long swallow and rose to leave. If he stayed there with her, he couldn't guarantee he wouldn't try to stroke her face again and again. No point in pushing things along too fast, not when it seemed he was finally making some headway.

❧

Rachel watched the door close behind him and touched the knife with a tender smile. How kind of him to take note of her fussing last night and sharpen it without saying a word. One corner of her mouth tilted upward. It appeared that Daniel felt the same way she did—if they were going to spend the rest of their lives as part of the same family, they might as well make sure they would be on good terms.

She wondered what he would have done to get into Pa's good graces if he were still alive. It wouldn't have been anything like sharpening a knife, she thought, chuckling. More like helping him break a horse or mend a wagon wheel.

And Pa would have been just as impressed as she felt. It showed that Daniel planned ahead and wanted a good relationship with his family-to-be. It also showed that she had read his intentions correctly. He wouldn't be doing this if he didn't plan to ask for Violet's hand.

That night after Daniel had gone home, the sisters sat before the fire, Rachel with her mending and Violet struggling with yarn and a pair of knitting needles.

"It's no good," Violet said, tossing the needles aside in disgust. "I'll never get the hang of knitting. It's a good thing you learned from Mother. Maybe you can teach me someday when we're old and gray and have nothing else to do." She looked at Rachel from under lowered lashes. "We can sit and talk about our grandchildren and what all our husbands have been up to."

Rachel suppressed a smile with an effort. What a way to lead up to the subject of marriage! Did her sister really think she didn't know which way the wind blew between her and Daniel? Fine, then. She would let Violet break the news in her own way, and she would show suitable surprise and delight when the moment came. She finished reattaching a dangling apron string and reached for another piece from the mending basket.

Violet worked to untangle her yarn and roll it back into a ball. "What do you think about Daniel?" she asked, her gaze never leaving her busy fingers.

Rachel tried not to snicker. She'd never realized Violet had such a gift for acting. If she didn't know better, she'd think her sister had no interest in the man at all. She toyed with the idea of sounding unenthusiastic but dismissed it. No point in teasing when something as important as her sister's future hung in the balance.

"I think he's a fine man," she responded, keeping her tone casual. "He's a hard worker, and he loves the Lord. Pretty good qualities, if you ask me." She pulled her stitches tight, waiting for Violet's next remark.

"That's good. I mean, you're right," Violet said. She wound the last wrap of yarn and tossed the ball into the sewing basket. "Those are important qualities for a man to have, don't you think? Important qualities for a husband, I mean."

"Absolutely." Rachel had to bite her lips to keep from laughing out loud. Violet couldn't be any more transparent if she tried.

"I'm glad." Violet took a deep breath and licked her lips. "Because he has feelings for you."

The needle slipped and jabbed Rachel in the thigh. "What?" she yelped.

"Isn't it wonderful?" Violet seemed oblivious to her sister's pained cry. "Assuming, of course, that you like him too," she added cautiously. "You do, don't you, Rachel?"

"Do—I—like—"

"You said yourself he's a fine man. Hard worker and God-fearing." She closed her eyes and heaved a blissful sigh. "It sounds like a match made in heaven to me."

Rachel rubbed the sore spot on her leg and tried to concentrate. What had happened to the announcement of Violet's intention to marry Daniel? She would have thought it all a dream, had it not been for the tender spot where the needle poked her. What about all those private conversations? Had he been toying with her sister's affections?

"Violet, don't you think I know how you feel about him? I hope you know I would never try to come between you." She had spent enough time on bended knees to know she meant every word.

Violet raised her eyebrows quizzically.

"Look at all the time you've spent with him," Rachel told her, mildly irked that her sister would force her to explain. "I've seen the looks passing back and forth between the two of you, all the smiles and the whispering." She gave Violet a reproving look. "You haven't been as unobtrusive as you think. It's pretty obvious."

Violet sprang to her feet. "Rachel, you goose! It isn't me he cares for. It never has been. It's you."

Rachel studied her sister's face, her heart beginning a wild flutter. Could it be true? Did the possibility exist that Daniel cared for her, Rachel Canfield? For herself and not the farm?

She dropped her mending in her lap and leaned back in her chair, staring at the wall but seeing Daniel's face. He'd put in so much hard effort, taking over the heavy labor of harvest for her, then staying on to work even more without any apparent reason. Then there was the way he'd looked at her earlier that day, and the thrill she'd felt when his hand touched her face not once, but twice.

Her head grew light. What if it were true? What if all the thoughtful gestures were meant for her as the object of his love rather than a potential sister-in-law whose goodwill he wanted to win?

Rachel closed her eyes, the better to picture their time together in the kitchen. She could recall every moment—his words, his smile, the tingle that shot through her arm when he'd handed her the knife and his fingertips touched hers.

Her lips curved in a gentle smile. Maybe dreams did come

true. Maybe God had decided to answer the deepest longings of her heart.

Without warning, another scene flashed before her eyes. She saw herself sitting at the table, explaining to Daniel that she was the sole owner of the property, that Violet had no legal interest in it whatsoever. Rachel jolted upright, the bitter taste of gall rising in her throat.

Of course he wanted her. She laughed in derision at her naivete, earning a puzzled look from Violet. He wanted her because she owned the land. She had been right about his intentions from the first. When he thought they both had rights to the property, pretty Violet had been the object of his attentions. Once he learned the truth, he switched his attention to Rachel without a moment's hesitation.

She pressed her hand to her mouth, fearing she might be sick. What made her think that Daniel, or any man, would want her? She wanted to howl out her anguish at her betrayal and even more at the realization that this new knowledge didn't change her feelings for Daniel in the least.

An idea took shape in her mind. Very well. If Daniel chose to play that game, she knew one way to find out his true motives, once and for all.

seventeen

He loved her. He loved her not. Rachel dropped the handful of straw to the ground, not having the heart to continue the childish game. Besides, loose straw made a poor substitute for the garden flowers she'd plucked petals from as a little girl in Missouri. But she had been hard-pressed to find any flowers blooming in the middle of December.

She stared across the yard, where the late afternoon had turned the snow into pools of slush. Dark gray clouds reappeared, and more snow drifted down into the puddles. It was a dismal day and a dismal scene. And Christmas was coming.

Her thoughts turned to Christmases past, times when her family didn't have a lot in the way of material goods but abounded in the richness of the joys of being together. This year the holiday looked as desolate as the landscape before her.

Pa had worked hard to keep the Christmas spirit alive even after their mother was gone, but now he too would be missing from the picture. It would be up to Rachel to carry on, and she didn't know if she could. Or whether she wanted to.

She shook herself, trying to cast off her downhearted mood. Hadn't she learned that God could be trusted, regardless of the circumstances? No matter what upheaval went on around them or within her emotions, she could experience joy, if she so chose, just in knowing His presence.

And He *was* there, she knew that for sure. Hadn't He given them help when they needed it most? Hadn't He blessed them with money over and above the amount she'd sought so desperately, even when she would have thought such a sum an utter impossibility? No matter what happened with Daniel, the Lord continued to be in control, she reminded herself, feeling a stirring of excitement. And she and Violet would celebrate His birth.

What could she do to make this Christmas especially nice for her sister? She felt compelled to make up for her surly attitude at Thanksgiving. A tree, she decided. Pa always sought out the perfect tree. Violet deserved some happiness, and she would provide it. She felt sure she could get Daniel to help cut one. She shrugged off a twinge of self-pity and set about making her plans.

What about gifts? Her pulse raced, realizing that with the money provided by the sale of the kittens, she would have a bit extra to buy something nice for Violet. With a light heart, she ran to hitch up the horses.

ෂ

Rachel browsed through the selection of goods in the general store, feeling positively giddy. How long had it been since she'd been able to shop for anything but the barest necessities?

Today she had money to spend, and she intended to enjoy the sensation. She didn't plan to throw it away, but after their extended time of deprivation, the mere thought of being able to pay for a tiny bit of luxury made for a heady experience.

She had already spotted some possibilities at the dry goods counter at the mercantile. Once she finished here, she would go back to buy some fabric and bits of ribbon for Violet to use to trim their tree.

"Made up your mind yet, Rachel?" Jake Samson's friendly smile let her know there was no impatience behind his words.

"I think so." She set her purchase on the counter. "I'd like this one. . .and a bag of peppermints, please." Her gaze lit on a shelf behind the counter, and she paused. "I'll take three of those handkerchiefs too," she told him, hoping he wouldn't ask who they were for.

"Here you go." He wrapped her items without so much as a flicker of interest and added up the total. Rachel counted out the money, happy to have spent even less than she expected.

She picked up her parcel and strolled toward the mercantile, then paused, changed direction, and went into the bank.

Ben Murphy looked up with a smile that told her he felt as relieved as she did that she no longer owed him money. "What can I do for you, Rachel?"

"Do you have those papers ready?"

The banker pulled a file from his desk drawer and stood, his brows knitted. "They're right here." He tapped the thin sheaf of papers slowly against his hand. "I drew them up just like you asked me to, but I don't underst—"

"It doesn't matter whether you understand or not," Rachel said crisply. "Just so they're legal and in order." She gave them a quick glance and nodded. "Merry Christmas, Ben," she told the perplexed banker and proceeded to the mercantile.

Back at home, she secreted Violet's present in her cupboard and tucked the handkerchiefs in the bottom dresser drawer, wondering if she'd been a fool to buy even that small gift for Daniel.

She found Violet in the kitchen and handed her the fabric and ribbon. "You'd better get started on this," she said in answer to her sister's puzzled frown. "We'll need decorations for the tree soon."

"A tree? Oh, Rachel!" Violet hugged her ecstatically. "I'd been so afraid. . .well, you know. This will make it a real Christmas, after all!"

Rachel returned the hug. "I'm glad it makes you happy. I'll

arrange for Daniel to take you out in the wagon, and you can make a day of picking out the prettiest tree you can find."

❧

Daniel showed up the next morning, bundled up in his heaviest coat. His face barely showed above the scarves wrapped around his neck. He strode into the kitchen, clapping his hands together to warm them. "Ready to go find a tree?" He looked at Violet expectantly.

She paused, and Rachel glanced up from polishing the lamp chimney, surprised at her sister's hesitation. "Actually, I was hoping to spend some time alone. Why don't you go, Rachel?"

Rachel opened her mouth to protest, but Violet took the rag from her hand and replaced the shiny glass globe on the base of the lamp.

"If you must know," Violet said, pulling Rachel's heavy work coat from its hook and prodding her sister toward the door, "I need to work on your Christmas present. . .when you aren't around."

She stuffed Rachel's limp arms into the sleeves as though she were a small child and gave her a maternal pat on the shoulder. "Scat. Go with Daniel, and don't come back until you've found the perfect tree. Go!" She flapped her hands in a shooing gesture as Rachel hovered uncertainly in the doorway.

Rachel shot a quick glance at Daniel, who just stood smiling, a bemused expression on his face. He looked a question at Violet, and Rachel turned quickly enough to intercept her sister's quick wink. Daniel pushed the door open and swept his arm out in a courtly gesture. "Your coach awaits."

What had passed between them? Rachel glared at Violet, then shoved a pair of gloves in her coat pocket and wound a scarf around her head.

Daniel tucked a lap robe firmly around Rachel and made sure she was settled before he snapped the reins and sent the horses off at a lively trot. Their hooves crunched in quick rhythm through the light crust of snow.

Rachel sat upright and stared straight ahead, achingly aware of Daniel's proximity. The last time they'd been together alone, they'd sat on opposite sides of the table. Now, mere inches separated them physically, but a gulf of doubt lay between them. For once in her life, Rachel couldn't think of a thing to say.

Daniel seemed to suffer from the same malady. He held the reins casually enough, but a quick peek from under her lowered lashes showed her his wary posture and stiff facial features. When he finally broke the silence, the sound of his voice made her jump.

"I thought we'd go out by Spruce Mountain to look at the trees there." He looked at her as if seeking her approval, and Rachel met his gaze directly for the first time since their encounter in the kitchen.

The clear sky, the forest, the snow-covered hills all seemed to slip away. The only scenery worth looking at was what she found in Daniel's deep green eyes.

His gaze probed hers intently as if asking a question she didn't know how to answer. Despite the bitter cold, she felt as though unseen sparks shot back and forth in the narrow gap between them.

Rachel shrank farther into the protection of her coat and clasped her gloved fingers tightly together beneath the shelter of the lap robe. With all her heart, she longed to reach out to caress his face, to trace with trembling fingers the lines of his full lips. In that moment, she could almost believe he felt the same.

"Is that all right with you?" He barely murmured the words,

but it was enough to break the tenuous spell that held them. Rachel felt as though she were awakening from a glorious dream.

"Is what all right?" She blinked her eyes, trying to recall what Daniel had asked.

A smile tugged at the corners of his mouth, causing Rachel's heart to race. "Going up to Spruce Mountain."

She nodded, then straightened her back, trying to pull herself together. Goodness! What had she been thinking? She'd never in her life gotten lost in someone's gaze like that. She must have looked like a lovesick calf. Blood rushed to her cheeks in a scalding blush. She'd better keep a tighter rein on her emotions and not let Daniel see how he affected her.

"Whoa." Daniel pulled the team to a halt at the edge of a clearing where stately pines towered over stands of oak and piñon and a scattering of spruce. "Here we are."

Rachel looked around dazedly. Had they reached the mountain already? If he said so. After five years of getting acquainted with this corner of the world, she had learned to tell her location at a glance. Today, she could have been plucked up by a giant hand and set down again in a foreign land, for all she knew. Her bearings had completely disappeared, swept away by the dizzying fact of Daniel's nearness.

He removed the lap robe, then jumped down from the seat and came around to assist Rachel. She stood on tottery legs and placed her hands on his shoulders. His broad hands encircled her waist, holding her in a grasp at once firm yet tender. He lifted her as easily as he would a shock of corn and swung her to the ground.

Had her perceptions been distorted by the wonder of this day, or did he really leave his hands clamped to her sides a moment longer than necessary? Rachel closed her eyes and breathed deeply to steady herself.

Daniel pulled an axe from the wagon bed and shouldered it, then reached for Rachel's hand. "Come on. Let's go find your tree."

The simple statement brought Rachel back to her senses. A gust of cold air nipped her cheeks and boosted her spirits. She had no idea what Daniel might be feeling at this moment or what the future might hold. In years to come, she might have only this one day to look back on with such fullness of delight. She would choose to enjoy it to its fullest. With that resolved in her mind, she clasped his proffered hand, and they set off together.

eighteen

Across the meadow and along the mountainside they wandered, careful not to slip on patches of ice in shady spots or trip over fallen branches buried in the snow. They examined, then rejected, any number of trees for one reason or another.

Rachel thought briefly of the farm and the chores she could have been doing, then dismissed them. Violet could handle things until she got back. She found an excuse to turn down even more trees in order to draw out their time together as long as possible.

"What about this one?" She followed the sound of Daniel's voice over the top of a low rise and found him standing before a six-foot spruce, admiring the spread of its branches.

"What do you think?" he asked. "It's not too tall for the house, but it's nice and full."

Rachel circled the tree, trying to picture it in place. She could see it standing proudly in the corner, wearing the decorations Violet had been working on all week. Her lips curved in a smile. "Perfect."

Daniel answered her smile with a broad grin and set to work with his axe. Rachel could see the strength of his shoulders in each powerful blow. A woman would never feel unprotected in those arms. She felt the hot rush of blood to her face even as the thought crossed her mind.

She tilted her head back to stare at the tallest of the trees, hoping Daniel would be so occupied with felling the spruce he wouldn't notice her reddened cheeks. Or maybe he would think it due to the cold.

She tried to set her mind on the tree, the weather, anything but Daniel and her attraction to him, but all her efforts came to naught. She could no more keep her thoughts away from him than she could fly. But what would one afternoon's daydreaming hurt? If it turned out that Daniel didn't love her, the memory of this one lovely day might be all she had to carry with her in memory throughout the lonely years ahead.

What had prompted Violet to voice the idea that Daniel might care for her? Rachel hadn't thought to ask when she first made her astounding disclosure and hadn't had the nerve later to bring up the subject herself. Her sister and Daniel did spend a goodly amount of time talking, but would he confide such private matters of the heart to her sister?

Probably not. More than likely, Violet had sailed off into one of her fantasy worlds again and fabricated the wild conjecture from some offhand comment Daniel had made that didn't mean anything of the kind.

She thought back over the past weeks, trying to recall anything that would give credence to Violet's theory. There had been numerous little kindnesses, but how many of those could be chalked up to acts of compassion for two young women trying to pull their lives together?

What about today? Daniel hadn't come seeking out her company, she remembered with a pang. It had been Violet's doing that they had this time together. But what of the tender expression in his eyes when their gazes locked and she'd felt like she were drowning in a sea of green? Or the lingering touch of his hands around her waist? Surely she hadn't imagined that.

"There she goes!" The tree began to topple, and Rachel scrambled out of the way. While Daniel went back to get the team, she tried to gain some control over her turbulent emotions. For all she knew, whatever interest there might be existed only on her part. It wouldn't help her peace of mind to let Violet's capricious imagination spark a risky train of thought that could crush her as easily as a falling tree.

She sat quiet on the ride home after Daniel had lashed the tree to the wagon. He tucked her in as tenderly as before, but Rachel kept well to her side of the seat and fixed her gaze determinedly on the road ahead. She wouldn't risk the luxury—the danger—of looking into those forest-green eyes again.

She felt as though she stood on the brink of a deep precipice, ready to teeter right over the edge. What had happened to her levelheadedness, the prudence that made her father willing to trust her with his property? All her reason seemed to vanish the moment she became vulnerable to Daniel's masculine appeal.

Her thoughts were interrupted when the wagon turned unexpectedly into the trees not far from Jeb McCurdy's land. Rachel blinked in confusion.

"I need to stop at home to pick something up," Daniel told her. "I hope you don't mind." He pulled up in a small clearing and leaped lightly from the seat. Rachel watched him hurry to a building that was nothing more than a glorified lean-to and duck into the doorway of the slapdash structure. Her lips parted in dismay. He called this place home? She stared around the property, looking for any sign of prosperity and finding none.

How could he have expected to redeem her from her money troubles? Cold fingers of misgiving clutched at her heart. If this run-down place gave any indication of his financial status, he was in a tighter fix than she and Violet.

"Got it." He returned to the wagon carrying a small bundle wrapped in burlap. Setting it behind the seat, he grinned and gave her a happy wink. "Ready?"

Rachel barely had time to nod before he shook the reins and headed out. She no longer wanted to believe he was only after the farm, but how could she think otherwise after the privation she'd just seen? The icy fingers squeezed her heart still harder.

☙

Violet opened the door with a glad cry of greeting. "Let me see what you've brought!" She circled the tree, her hands clasped with delight, and exclaimed over its even shape.

They dragged it inside and set it up across the room from the fireplace. Violet produced her handmade ornaments, and they all helped adorn the tree. When the last bow had been hung, Rachel went to heat water for tea while Violet admired their handiwork.

Daniel excused himself and went out to the barn. He returned with a burlap-wrapped object in his hand. "This is what I stopped for," he told Rachel with unaccustomed diffidence. "I thought you might be able to use it."

She took the parcel from him, careful not to meet his gaze, and peeled off the protective layers. An angel, wings spread and face lifted in adoration, lay in her hands. "Wherever did you get this?" she asked wonderingly.

Daniel shrugged self-consciously. "Carved it from a piece of oak. A man's got to have something to do with his hands besides chop wood and push a plow." He pointed to a cavity whittled into the base. "You can set it on the top branch, if you like."

Rachel turned the wooden figure this way and that, admiring its delicate lines, then held it out to Daniel. "Would you put it up, please?" His fingers brushed hers when he took the angel back, and again she felt the familiar tingle run up her arms.

She steadied a chair for him to climb on to set the angel on the uppermost branch. He took his time positioning it just so, making sure the figure stood upright. Violet clapped her hands when he had finished, and Rachel felt a rush of admiration.

"Guess I'd better leave," Daniel said, picking up his hat.

Violet's brow crinkled. "Won't you stay for supper? After all, you spent a lot of time helping us get the tree."

Rachel's anxiety mounted while she waited for him to answer. After their splendid day together, she knew she would feel bereft if he decided to leave now.

"Better not," he said. "I have some things to do back at my place."

Rachel threw a shawl across her shoulders and followed him out to the porch, unwilling to let the connection she had felt be broken. "Thank you for all your help," she told him. "Getting that tree has made it a wonderful occasion for Violet. For both of us," she added, lowering her eyes.

"I enjoyed doing it," he told her, his voice husky in the clear evening air. "I enjoyed the company too." He raised his hand to her face, one finger trailing along her cheek to tuck a stray wisp of hair behind her ear.

Rachel caught her breath in a ragged gulp, conscious of his nearness, his warmth. She knew Violet was just inside the house, but it felt as though the two of them stood alone in the stillness of the eventide. She tilted her head back to search his face, hoping to find some hint of caring.

Daniel's hand cupped her face, and she pressed her cheek into the soft caress. He leaned so close his breath stirred the loose wisps of hair at her temples. "Rachel," he whispered.

She stared at him wordlessly, filled with a yearning beyond her powers to express.

He closed his eyes and shook his head, slowly withdrawing his hand. "Another time." He took two steps backward, not breaking their linked gazes until he turned and walked away.

Rachel stood gazing into the twilight long after the receding echo of his horse's hooves told her Daniel had gone. The evening chill permeated the scant protection of her shawl. She shivered and went into the house.

Later, she stared at her bedroom ceiling from her warm cocoon of blankets and wondered. What had he been about to say? His tone and abrupt departure made it seem like he'd interrupted a confession. But of what—love or deceit?

She twisted into a different position under the sheet, wishing she knew his heart. If only he cared for her. She moaned and pulled the pillow over her head. No use getting carried away by dreams of something that might not exist.

&

A log crackled and settled into the fire, sending a shower of sparks up the chimney. The burst of light illumined the lovingly decorated tree across the room. Rachel took a final stitch and bit off the end of the thread. The embroidered initials stood out clearly, even in the firelight: DWM. Daniel Webster Moore. She traced the letters, calling herself a lovesick fool.

When she had asked Jake Samson to add the handkerchiefs to her order, she'd told herself they were only to show Daniel some token of appreciation for all the hard work he had done. It was a good thing she'd decided to work on these after Violet had gone to bed, she thought, folding the handkerchiefs into neat squares. No matter what protestations of unconcern she might make, her sister would have seen right through her supposed indifference.

Handkerchiefs, to her mind, had been a safe choice. They showed she valued his hard months of labor but didn't give any indication of sentiment. The idea of giving Daniel a gift of thanks made perfect sense to her, even now. Spending the past two evenings embellishing them with her neatest stitches didn't.

She placed her needle and thread in the sewing basket and wrapped the kerchiefs in a scrap of calico, tying the parcel securely with string. After a moment's consideration, she bent to tuck the small package beneath the Christmas tree. It could wait for Daniel there until sometime after the holiday. Christmas Day would be just for her and Violet. After the way she had behaved over the past few months, a quiet day with just the two of them would help to make amends.

nineteen

"How can you not want to invite Daniel to dinner tomorrow?" Violet's eyes were wide blue pools of astonishment. "He's done so much for us!"

"Granted. But Christmas should be a family time. We've both worked hard, and I know I haven't always been easy to get along with. Tomorrow is *our* day, Violet."

"Where's your sense of fair play? You can't make him spend the day all alone. Please, Rachel, it's Christmas Eve!" Violet wrung her hands and danced from one foot to the other, looking for all the world like a child begging for a coveted treat.

"No, my mind's made up. I want time with just you."

Violet flung her hands in the air and stalked into the kitchen, muttering about ingratitude.

Rachel rolled her eyes. Why couldn't her sister enjoy the idea of the two of them having a relaxing day in each other's company? Sometimes she didn't understand Violet, didn't understand her at all. She opened her mouth to argue further, but a knock at the door interrupted her.

She swung it wide, to be greeted by a mass of dark feathers hanging at eye level. "What on earth—"

Daniel's grinning face peeked around the massive turkey. "I heard a bunch of gobblers out back of my place early this morning, so I grabbed my rifle and went looking. Quite a specimen, isn't he?" He hoisted the bird admiringly.

Violet hurried from the kitchen. "Goodness, what a huge bird!"

"I thought you might like to have him for Christmas dinner," Daniel said. "I'll pluck him and get him ready out back."

"What a lovely idea!" Violet gushed, darting a meaningful glance at Rachel. "How thoughtful of you to want to make our Christmas perfect." She dug an elbow into Rachel's ribs.

Rachel flinched and rubbed her side. "All right," she muttered between clenched teeth. "You win." Raising her voice, she called, "Would you like to have Christmas dinner with us? We'll eat about one o'clock." She managed a smile for Daniel, then turned to glare daggers at Violet. Honestly! Some people just didn't make it a bit easy to do anything nice for them.

Her annoyance melted away when she thought of a whole day in Daniel's company, with only minimal chores to claim her time.

❧

Daniel tossed down the last handful of turkey feathers. Normally he hated everything about the messy job, but today he couldn't help but grin. Providing the main course for Christmas dinner had insured him of an invitation to join the Canfield sisters at their holiday meal, just as Violet predicted.

He shook his head in admiration. The girl knew her sister, all right. And she'd proved to be a quick thinker. Her idea of pushing Rachel into hunting for their tree at the last minute had taken him by surprise, but he'd caught her conspiratorial nod and played along with her strategy.

Good thing too. Look how well that had turned out. If he hadn't read the signs wrong, Rachel had been as sorry to end their day together as he'd been. He smiled, remembering the way she'd followed him outside. If he hadn't caught himself just in time, he might have jumped the gun and proposed out on the porch that night instead of following their strategy.

He only hoped the plans they'd laid for tomorrow ran as smoothly as Violet expected them to.

❧

The earth wore a new coating of snow Christmas morning, giving the whole area a sparkling look of anticipation. Rachel felt that same sense of expectation mirrored in her heart all the while she set bread out to rise, prepared the dressing, and stuffed the turkey.

Daniel would be coming for dinner. The thought sent shivers of excitement along her arms, followed by a quick twinge of guilt. This was the very reason she'd wanted to have the day alone with Violet. If Daniel was anywhere nearby, her attention would be on him and not her sister.

Speaking of Violet. . .Rachel listened at her bedroom door, but the even breathing from under the blankets assured her that Violet still slept. Rachel tiptoed back to the kitchen. If nothing else, she could at least let her sleep late this morning.

She slid the bird into the oven and looked around, taking stock. Nothing remained to be done just now. Time enough later to wake Violet and let her help peel potatoes and roll out pie crusts. Until then, Rachel had a few precious moments to herself.

She exchanged her apron for her coat, then poured a cup of coffee and slipped outside, closing the door quietly behind her. Steam from the mug swirled before her eyes, then rose to join the dull gray clouds hanging overhead. Rachel sipped the fragrant brew and closed her eyes in pleasure. It had been far too long since she'd had time to savor a peaceful moment like this.

She opened her eyes again and surveyed the tranquil scene, determined to enjoy every bit of this blissful respite. To the north, Granite Mountain dominated the landscape, its frosty mantle flowing down its slopes and spreading out across the rugged land, stretching all the way to where she sat. The clean white blanket shimmered before her; only the tracks of tiny nocturnal wanderers marred its pristine surface.

She filled her lungs with the clear mountain air, refreshing as the purest spring water. Her heart overflowed with contentment, and a wellspring of gratitude for the breathtaking beauty of the place she called home flooded her soul.

Scuffing sounds from the kitchen alerted her to the fact that Violet had awakened. She hurried inside. Violet stood in the kitchen doorway in her white nightdress, tousled dark hair falling around her shoulders in unruly waves. She shifted from one bare foot to another, excited as a little girl. "It's Christmas!" she cried and ran to give Rachel a hug.

Rachel returned her embrace with fervor, breathing a quick prayer of thanks for God's grace in bringing them through the year's trials. Then she held Violet at arm's length and studied her. "You'd better go wash that sleep from your eyes and get dressed before Daniel comes, Lazybones."

Violet made a face but hurried to comply. "Do you want to exchange gifts now or later?" she called over her shoulder.

Thinking of the three wrapped handkerchiefs under the tree made Rachel's stomach lurch. "Let's wait until after dinner." Maybe by then she'd have worked up the nerve to give them to him.

≈

Daniel dampened a cloth in his basin and used it to brush down his suit coat and pants. He stood back, checking it carefully for wrinkles. There. That should do it.

When Violet had questioned him about his wardrobe the week before, he'd told her he had some nice clothes back at his cabin at the claim without a second thought. He hadn't expected her order to make the long trip over in the snow to retrieve them, though. He'd grumbled all the way over and back, but he'd followed her directive, just the same. Hadn't she been right about everything so far? It wouldn't make sense to ignore her advice this close to achieving his goal.

He dressed, wishing he had a decent looking glass to check his appearance in. He didn't consider himself a vain man, but an occasion like this demanded he look his best.

"Lord, I'm really going to need Your help today." He wet his hands and slicked back his hair. "I believe this is what You want, what You've led me to, and I'll admit it sounds mighty good to me. Rachel may take some convincing, though. Soften her heart, Lord, and make her see Your will."

With a last glance in his cracked shaving mirror, he gathered his things together and walked out the door.

twenty

"More potatoes?" Violet offered the heavy bowl to their guest with a sweet smile. Rachel cast a furtive glance at Daniel, trying to reconcile the sight of him today with the plain-dressed workingman she was used to.

What a picture he made today! She'd become so accustomed to seeing him in a flannel work shirt and canvas pants that when he showed up on their doorstep in a starched shirt with a wing collar, she almost didn't recognize him. She sneaked another look. Her heart hadn't resumed its normal pace since he walked in wearing a double-breasted Chesterfield and doffed his bowler hat.

Rachel reached to pass the gravy boat to Violet and saw Daniel watching her. Again. She took a deep breath to calm herself and hoped the gravy wouldn't slosh and betray her trembling hands. Much as she took pleasure in Daniel's company and lighthearted holiday conversation, the knowledge that his eyes seldom focused on anything but her had been unnerving.

She picked up her fork and speared her last bite of turkey. If she concentrated on eating, maybe no one would notice her lack of contribution to the dinner table conversation.

"You're awfully quiet." Violet's innocent comment dashed her hopes of going undetected.

She summoned up a smile. "Just enjoying this delicious bird, I guess." She rose to clear away the dishes, but Violet jumped to her feet.

"Let me do that, Rachel." She colored under her older sister's surprised scrutiny but didn't back down. "Sit still and relax for a change. It *is* Christmas, after all." With a clanking of crockery that made Rachel shudder, she carted off an armload of dishes.

Rachel resumed her seat and tried to think of something to say to break the uneasy silence. She felt her face grow warm. They hadn't been given to doing much entertaining, but surely she ought to be able to do better than this. Violet returned for another load of dishes, but she didn't expect much help from that quarter. What would Pa have talked about if he were here today? Her mind fumbled around for likely topics.

"Did you get enough to eat?" The moment the words left her mouth, she knew how inane they probably sounded. Violet's eye-rolling grimace and the flicker of amusement in Daniel's eyes confirmed her fears, and she writhed in mortification. Violet left again, shaking her head.

"You ladies did yourselves proud with that meal. I can't remember when I've eaten as well."

Rachel gave Daniel an appreciative look, letting her gaze linger on his face.

Violet reentered the room. "Time to open our gifts," she said, clapping her hands like a schoolteacher calling her class to attention.

At the thought of the handkerchiefs she'd embroidered for Daniel, Rachel's mouth grew dry, and her stomach churned. She should never have bought them in the first place. Would he read into her gesture more than she intended? Worse, would he be able to read into it everything that *was* there—her hopes, her dreams, her longings?

She pressed her hands to her cheeks and commanded herself to calm down. How ridiculous to carry on like that over something that probably wouldn't matter to him in the least.

He would see the handkerchiefs as a gracious gesture provided by a thoughtful hostess, she assured herself, not a smitten woman's attempt to gain attention. They might even have been some of Pa's that she had pulled out at the last minute. Except that Pa's initials hadn't been DWM, she reminded herself, wiping her damp palms against her skirt.

Seating herself in the rocking chair, she lifted her chin and tried to appear unconcerned. What if he did realize she'd bought and monogrammed them just for him? He didn't have to know that all the longing of her heart had gone into every stitch.

"Who wants to go first?" Violet looked around with a bright smile. Rachel stirred uneasily, aware that at some point her younger sister had usurped her duties as hostess. "All right, Daniel, you start." She pulled a lumpy package from behind her chair and placed it in his hands.

Daniel turned the odd-shaped piece over in his hands, a bemused smile on his face. "I hope you aren't expecting me to guess what this is," he said.

Violet laughed delightedly. Rachel stared at the package, mystified. It bore no resemblance to anything she could imagine, with numerous protuberances angling up from a flat base.

Daniel pulled off the brown paper wrapping to reveal a horn mounted on a board. He held it aloft and squinted at it.

"It's a hat rack," Violet informed him proudly. "I made it from a shed deer antler I found." She grinned and added, "You're holding it upside down."

Daniel quickly reversed the contraption. "A hat rack, eh? And a fine one too." He leaned it up against the wall, where it tottered precariously. "Thank you, Violet. It was thoughtful of you to go to all that trouble."

Rachel closed her eyes in relief. *Thoughtful.* That's how he would see her gift too. A thoughtful remembrance, nothing more.

Violet scanned the small group of gifts under the tree and selected one wrapped in burlap. "I'll open this one." She unrolled the coarse fabric and squealed in delight. "Look, Rachel, it's Molly!" She held up a wooden carving for her inspection. "Oh, thank you, Daniel, it's adorable!"

"I don't know when you found the time to work on that and the tree angel," Rachel told him, examining the figure. "It's a wonderful likeness. You really do have a gift for this."

She handed the carved cat back to Violet, trying to hide her agitation. So Daniel had taken time to make presents for them? Then it was probably a good thing she had a gift for him. Embroidering his initials hadn't taken nearly as much time as carving a wooden figure, though. She just hoped her offering would be adequate.

Her imagination wandered while Violet sorted through the remaining presents. Daniel had obviously taken pains to come up with an idea that had special meaning for Violet. What could he have made for her? A voice penetrated her happy speculation, and she realized Violet was talking to her.

"Here." Her sister passed her a brown paper package. Her blue gaze held excitement and a bit of nervousness. "This one's from me."

Rachel fingered the flat square, trying to guess what it might be. Giving up, she tore off the paper wrapping and stared openmouthed at the intricate sampler within.

"Do you like it?" Violet asked doubtfully.

"Oh, Honey, it's wonderful." Rachel examined the delicate needlework. A vine wove its way through a border of dainty spring flowers surrounding the words "In everything give thanks." The words taken from Paul's second epistle to the Thessalonians spoke to her heart in a deeper way than ever before. Hadn't her heavenly Father been teaching her just that lesson through all her trials? Her eyes misted over, and she blinked back the tears. "I'll treasure it always."

Violet's smile was radiant. "We've gone around once," she announced, "so we'll let Daniel open his other gift. I think this is from Rachel."

She handed him the small package, and Rachel felt her heart begin a wild pounding. Would he think the gift foolish or overly sentimental? She barely breathed, watching him undo the string and pull open the calico wrapping.

Daniel spread the handkerchiefs open on his knee and traced the embroidered initials on each one with a work-calloused finger. He kept silent a long moment, then turned to Rachel with a solemn expression. "Thank you," he said simply. "You must have worked hard on these."

Rachel let her breath out in a whoosh. He hadn't seemed put off at all! Lightheaded with relief, she suddenly realized she was enjoying the day immensely.

She turned her attention back to Violet. While her sister studied her wood carving from Daniel more closely, Rachel did a mental inventory. Daniel had opened presents from both her and Violet.

Violet set down the little cat and prepared to open her second present, the one from Rachel. Rachel's stomach fluttered with excitement. Her gift from Daniel would be next. Giddy with anticipation, she could hardly wait to see what it would contain.

"Oh!" Violet had opened the box and withdrew a delicate gold chain supporting a heart-shaped locket.

"Open it," Rachel told her quietly. She watched her sister

pry the locket apart and stare at the tiny photographs within. The tears welling in Violet's eyes told her she'd gone a long way toward atoning for her grumpy behavior by splurging on this gift.

"Ma's and Pa's pictures," Violet whispered, pressing the necklace to her chest. "I can't think of anything I'd like more than this."

Rachel basked in the warm glow of contentment that washed over her. Despite her earlier misgivings, this Christmas had turned out to be far more wonderful than she'd ever imagined. She looked at Violet expectantly, ready to open her last gift.

Violet gave her a blank look, then stared around the bottom of her chair and under the tree. "I guess that's all," she cried gaily. "Hasn't this been a lovely day?"

Disappointment wrenched at Rachel's heart. Just when she was ready to open herself to Daniel and dare to believe he might reciprocate her feelings, her expectations had toppled and fallen with a crash. The letdown made her feel as though she'd stepped off a cliff and would never hit bottom.

She stared unseeingly for a moment, then jumped to her feet, determined not to give the others any reason to suspect the bitterness of the blow she'd received. "Let's have our dessert now," she said, trying to inject a merry note into her quavering voice.

"Not just yet," Violet said. "I want to run out to the barn for a bit and take some scraps to Molly." She yanked her coat from its hook and answered Rachel's incredulous look with a cheery smile. "She deserves a treat too. It's Christmas." She grabbed a turkey wing, looked meaningfully at Daniel, and hurried out.

Rachel stared at the closed door in disbelief. Wishing a

happy Christmas to a cat? What had gotten into Violet? Being alone with Daniel just then was the last thing she wanted.

She cast about for some way to busy herself and went to fetch the pies. She would go ahead and dish up dessert while Violet was gone. It would give her something to do, something that didn't require looking at him and wondering what he could be thinking. Keeping active would help her hide her aching heart.

Moving to the sideboard, she selected three plates. She turned to carry them to the table. . .and bumped right into Daniel. The plates rattled in her unsteady grasp, and Daniel placed his hands on hers. Taking the dishes from her, he set them on the sideboard and recaptured her hands.

Rachel tried to pull them away but couldn't make herself move. Every muscle in her body seemed to have lost its ability to respond to her mind's commands. She stared into Daniel's face, drinking in his nearness and willing her feet to put some distance between them. She couldn't keep her guard up much longer, then he'd be able to read the truth in her eyes. If she didn't move now, right now, she was in fearful danger of making a terrible fool of herself.

Turn your head. Look away! her mind screamed, but she could no more tear her fingers from his gentle grasp than reclaim her heart.

Daniel's hands slid up past her wrists and over her sleeves, following the contours of her arms until they came to rest on her shoulders. The color of his eyes deepened, turning them almost to black. Rachel had to remind herself to breathe.

"We need to talk," he said, his voice barely above a whisper. His thumbs traced slow circles on her upper arms. "I once made you an offer. The right offer, it turns out, but for all the wrong reasons." He moistened his lips and leaned closer.

"Do you remember? I told you I wanted to marry you. Like a fool, I was so puffed up with grand ideas of chivalry that I only saw it as a means of simplifying things for us both. I didn't see until later that if I didn't have you in my life, I'd be missing out on the most wonderful gift God could ever give me."

She stood motionless, feeling the gentle pressure of his fingers on her shoulder blades and wondering how she should respond. Weren't these the very words she'd longed to hear? Why couldn't she give in to the cry of her heart and allow herself to trust him?

Her thoughts turned to the papers in the sideboard. Could she bear to produce them now? With all her being, she wanted nothing more than to proclaim her love for him, but she had to know the truth.

Shaky with emotion, she moved to the sideboard and drew the papers from their hiding place. "Before we go any further, I think you should look at these." Her voice shook, but she stood firm.

Daniel took the papers, his forehead creased in bewilderment. "What's this?"

Rachel cleared her throat, hating herself for admitting her doubts, but knowing she had to force herself to go through with it. "I had them drawn up at the bank. They give the house, the farm, everything to Violet. She'll have sole possession." She watched him scan the first page and waited for his reaction. If he wanted only the land, this would change his attitude in a hurry.

He tossed the papers aside and regarded her with an expression of infinite regret. She stiffened, preparing for the blow to come. "Oh, Rachel," he breathed and reached for her again. "You just had to make sure, didn't you?" A smile twisted the corners of his mouth, and he drew a deep breath.

"In a way, I'm glad you did this so there'll never be any uncertainty in your mind. I love you, Rachel. *You,* not this property. I'd have been glad to farm it and build it up, knowing what it means to you, but I'll be just as happy to start over anywhere you want. . .as long as I have you."

She repeated his words over and over in her mind before comprehension fully dawned on her. Then a joyful trembling began in her fingertips and spread through her whole body. He loved her. Her, Rachel Canfield, with all her foolishness and flaws! She roused from her daze to realize Daniel had taken hold of her shoulders once more.

"Now that you know what my true feelings are, let me try this again." He drew a solemn breath. "I love you and everything about you—your strength, your courage, your faith in God—all the things that make you the amazing woman you are. I couldn't ask for a better helpmate. Rachel, will you marry me?"

She opened her lips to answer but couldn't form the words. Instead she nodded her head, slowly at first, then more quickly as tears of joy spilled down her cheeks. "Yes," she breathed, the words bursting forth at last. "Yes, Daniel, I will marry you!"

One sun-bronzed hand slid behind her shoulders to caress her neck while the other moved to cradle her cheek. With infinite tenderness, Daniel pulled her to him, gazing intently into her eyes. "Know this, Rachel Canfield. I'm well aware of my faults, but one thing you can be certain of. No matter what may come our way, you can trust me, now and forever." Tightening his embrace, he lowered his face and covered her mouth with his.

Rachel closed her eyes and felt her arms creep up past his shoulders to twine themselves around his neck. Her fears crumbled and fell away, lost in the joy of the certainty of Daniel's love.

Long moments later he pulled away, still holding her close. "I have something for you." He reached into his pocket with one hand and produced a faded velvet box, opening it to reveal a gold band set with a small diamond.

"This belonged to my father's mother." He slipped it on her finger and sealed it in place with a kiss. "Merry Christmas, my love."

Rachel's gaze rested on the handkerchiefs. "I didn't get you much," she told him with a catch in her voice.

"You're wrong," he said, brushing his lips across her forehead. "You've just promised me the greatest gift I could imagine. . .yourself, for a lifetime."

She raised her face and lost herself in another lingering kiss.

Daniel cupped her face in both his hands and smiled at her tenderly. "So, where do you want to live once we're married?"

Rachel colored in embarrassment and dropped her gaze to the floor. A moment later, she looked up, shamefaced. "How about right here?" she asked sheepishly.

Daniel tilted his head and lifted one eyebrow.

She picked up the sheaf of papers and opened it to the last page. "I only had them drawn up. . .they've never been signed."

A look of incredulity flooded Daniel's face, then he threw back his head and laughed. "Rachel, Rachel. Life with you will never grow dull." He wrapped his arms around her and squeezed her tight. "I promise I'll do my best to make this the finest farm in the Territory and provide a good home for you and Violet. . .and our children," he added softly, stroking her cheek with his knuckles.

Rachel pressed her head against his chest and melted into

his warm embrace. A tap on the door roused her, and she turned to see Violet poke her head inside.

"Are you two about finished?" she asked through chattering teeth. "I've done everything I can possibly think of to do outside, and it's freezing out here."

twenty-one

"Is everything in place?" Rachel pressed her hands to her face. "My mind is in such a whirl I can't think straight."

"You're doing just fine," Violet assured her, spreading a white cloth across the table and smoothing out its snowy folds. "And yes, we're nearly ready." She stepped back, eyed the cloth critically, and reached out to straighten one corner. "There." She smiled in satisfaction. "Doesn't that look nice?"

Rachel nodded distractedly. "The food—is it ready? I can't remember if I took the bread out of the oven or not. And what about the decorations?"

With a patient sigh, Violet took her by the shoulder and turned her around to face the room. "Just look at it, Rachel. The house is lovely. Don't worry, everything is going to be fine."

"Fine," Rachel repeated, trying to absorb her sister's words. She forced herself to concentrate and scanned the room. Richly colored bows, fashioned by Violet from pieces of fabric she'd discovered in an old trunk, festooned the walls. An arrangement of pinecones and evergreen boughs held a place of honor atop the mantel. And over in the corner stood the Christmas tree, lending its air of regal beauty to the scene.

"Fine," she said again. It did look nice. She relaxed a fraction, then she thought of the kitchen. "The bread!" she cried, whirling to run check the oven.

Violet caught her arm and held her in a firm grasp. "I took

the bread out twenty minutes ago. It looks wonderful." She held up a hand to cut off further protests. "The venison is roasting now, and I've put the potatoes and carrots on to boil. The whole meal will be done to perfection, and you don't need to worry about a thing." She emphasized the last words with a jab of her finger.

"Trust me, Rachel. Everything will be ready well before the guests arrive. I've even made a cake," she said smugly.

Rachel stared at her sister through eyes that didn't want to focus. When had they traded places, with Violet taking over the role of the down-to-earth counselor? She shook her head to clear it but only succeeded in making it throb.

"Relax," Violet told her, wrapping her arms around her in a comforting hug. "You're just tired. It's a lot of work putting a wedding together in a week."

Rachel returned the hug, appreciating the emotional lifeline. Had it been a week since Daniel proposed for the second time, the time that took her breath away and sent her into this state of rapturous confusion? Sometimes it seemed like only a moment had passed, other times she felt as though he'd been woven into the fabric of her life forever.

And maybe he had, she mused. Maybe the sense of completeness she now felt came as the result of finally finding a part of herself she hadn't realized was missing.

She pulled away and turned to survey their preparations one more time, unable to believe they'd been able to pull everything together in a mere matter of days. Try as she might, she couldn't find a thing out of place. Violet was right; she needed to relax and enjoy this day of days.

The image of Daniel's dear face formed in her mind. She remembered the feeling of his strong arms around her as he took his leave the night before. "I know a week hasn't given you much time to get ready," he whispered, his lips grazing her ear. "But without a lot of family to plan for, there just didn't seem to be much point in waiting any longer."

He tilted her face up to meet his smiling gaze. "Besides, I like the idea of starting out a brand-new year as man and wife."

"Rachel?" Violet's insistent tap on her shoulder interrupted her reverie. "I said to relax, not fall asleep. You'd better start thinking about getting dressed."

With a startled glance at the mantel clock, Rachel hurried to her room. There on her bed lay the treasure Violet had found while digging through trunks for more decorations. The yellowed satin of their mother's wedding dress spread across her comforter in flowing lines.

A lump formed in her throat, and she blinked back sudden tears. "I wish you could have been here on this day, Ma. You and Pa both. It would have been good to have you with me." But maybe they knew of her newfound happiness; maybe they were watching from the portals of heaven even now. The thought cheered her, and she raised her hands to undo the buttons on her dress.

"Need any help?" Violet slipped into the room and lent a hand with the buttons, then lifted the wedding dress reverently. It slid over Rachel's head and shoulders in a rush of satiny smoothness. Violet fastened each tiny button up the back, then stood back and looked at her sister with awe.

"You're beautiful," she whispered. She hurried to tilt the looking glass so Rachel could see her reflection.

Violet was right, she thought in stunned wonder. Love for Daniel shone in her face, giving her a radiance she had never dreamed possible. A knock at the front door jarred her back to the present.

"Fix your hair." Violet thrust a hairbrush in her hand and hurried from the room. "I'll let you know when it's time."

The scuffle of boots in the front of the house told her their guests had arrived. Through the commotion, she heard the voice of the minister from town. Thank goodness. They could manage a wedding without guests, but the preacher was a necessity. In another moment, Daniel's deep baritone filtered into the room. Rachel closed her eyes and sighed. The minister was there; Daniel was there. Everything would be all right.

Her door opened and closed again, and Violet stood before her, eyes sparkling with excitement. "Ready?"

"I think so." Rachel drew a shaky breath and smiled at her sister. "Someday you'll be wearing this dress."

Violet returned her smile and squeezed her hands. "That someday may be a long way off. Right now, you have a very handsome man waiting for you out there. Let's go."

Rachel nodded and followed her sister from the room. She searched the happy faces that turned to greet her: Ben Murphy, Jake Samson and his wife, two unfamiliar men she assumed must be Abner and Seth Watson. Not a large number of onlookers, but people who were dear to her and Daniel.

Beyond them, a lone figure stood silhouetted in the doorway. Rachel strained to make out who it was, then felt a quick flush rise to her cheeks when she recognized the grinning face of Jeb McCurdy.

She moved past their guests, her step hesitating when she finally glimpsed the one person her eyes had sought. Daniel stood before the fireplace, waiting. Waiting for her. The next moment, she clasped his fingers in her own, standing at his side before the little group as she would from this day forward.

The minister cleared his throat. "We are gathered here

today in the sight of God and these witnesses," he began, "to join this couple in holy matrimony."

Over Daniel's shoulder, she could see the angel atop the tree, seeming to assure her that heaven saw and blessed their union.

"Daniel, do you take this woman to be your lawfully wedded wife?"

The forest-green gaze drew her into its depths. "I do."

"Rachel, do you take this man to be your lawfully wedded husband?"

She tightened her fingers around the hands of the man she loved. Strong hands, good hands. "I do," she whispered.

"Then repeat after me. . ." His words and Daniel's reply faded into the distance as she thought about God's unsearchable goodness, the unbelievable blessings He had bestowed on her. Daniel gave her hands a squeeze, and she realized the minister looked at her expectantly.

"I, Rachel, take thee, Daniel," she repeated obediently. *My wonderful Daniel, my other half.*

"To be my husband. . ." *I'll be the best wife I know how.*

"To have and to hold from this day forward, for better for worse, for richer for poorer, in sickness and in health. . ." *The Lord has seen us through this time of testing. He'll be with us in whatever comes our way.*

"To love, honor, and obey, until death do us part." She spoke the final words, almost certain that somewhere her parents wept for joy.

"You may kiss the bride."

Daniel raised his hands, placing one on each side of her face. Slowly, he bent toward her, and she raised her lips to his, melting into his kiss and floating away on a cloud of pure joy.

When they parted at last, Rachel smiled at the sound of the

guests' applause but didn't remove her gaze from Daniel's face. The face of her husband. She marveled at the thought.

Her spirit sent a joyful shout of praise to heaven. God had not only seen her through her darkest hour but added in the unexpected gift of Daniel's love.

The time of sorrow had passed, giving way to a season of hope.

A Letter To Our Readers

Dear Reader:

In order that we might better contribute to your reading enjoyment, we would appreciate your taking a few minutes to respond to the following questions. We welcome your comments and read each form and letter we receive. When completed, please return to the following:

Rebecca Germany, Fiction Editor
Heartsong Presents
PO Box 719
Uhrichsville, Ohio 44683

1. Did you enjoy reading *Season of Hope* by Carol Cox?
    ❑ Very much! I would like to see more books
    by this author!
    ❑ Moderately. I would have enjoyed it more if

    _____

    _____

    _____

2. Are you a member of **Heartsong Presents**?   Yes ❑ No ❑
    If no, where did you purchase this book? _____

    _____

3. How would you rate, on a scale from 1 (poor) to 5 (superior), the cover design? _____

4. On a scale from 1 (poor) to 10 (superior), please rate the following elements.

    _____ Heroine   _____ Plot

    _____ Hero   _____ Inspirational theme

    _____ Setting   _____ Secondary characters

5. These characters were special because_____

_____

_____

6. How has this book inspired your life?_____

_____

_____

7. What settings would you like to see covered in future
   Heartsong Presents books?_____

_____

_____

8. What are some inspirational themes you would like to see
   treated in future books?_____

_____

_____

9. Would you be interested in reading other **Heartsong
   Presents** titles?   Yes ❏   No ❏

10. Please check your age range:
    ❏ Under 18   ❏ 18-24   ❏ 25-34
    ❏ 35-45   ❏ 46-55   ❏ Over 55

Name _____

Occupation _____

Address _____

City _____ State _____ Zip _____

Email _____

Texas

*T*he late 1880s are prosperous times for East Texas ranches and cattle towns. But Dogwood, Texas, seems to be plagued with emotional and physical dangers, especially for four women thrown into the arms of high adventure and unexpected love.

When the going gets rough, these resilient women struggle with turning their backs on love or trusting God to see them through. Discover the intrigue, the adventure, the romance of the South, and the charm of the past in four complete novels from acclaimed author Debra White Smith.

paperback, 464 pages, 5 ³/₁₆" x 8"

·······Presents·······

Hearts♥ng Presents
Love Stories Are Rated G!

That's for godly, gratifying, and of course, great! If you love a thrilling love story but don't appreciate the sordidness of some popular paperback romances, **Heartsong Presents** is for you. In fact, **Heartsong Presents** is the *only inspirational romance book club* featuring love stories where Christian faith is the primary ingredient in a marriage relationship.

Sign up today to receive your first set of four never-before-published Christian romances. Send no money now; you will receive a bill with the first shipment. You may cancel at any time without obligation, and if you aren't completely satisfied with any selection, you may return the books for an immediate refund!

Imagine. . .four new romances every four weeks—two historical, two contemporary—with men and women like you who long to meet the one God has chosen as the love of their lives. . .all for the low price of $9.97 postpaid.

To join, simply complete the coupon below and mail to the address provided. **Heartsong Presents** romances are rated G for another reason: They'll arrive *Godspeed!*